MW00947663

THE ADVENTURES OF ABIGAIL

RHYTHM OF THE ICEBERG

By

Yolanda Boone, M.S. CCC-SLP

Copyright © 2018 by Yolanda Boone, M.S.CCC-SLP

All rights reserved. This book or any portion thereof may not be reproduced or used in any manner whatsoever without the express written permission of the publisher except for the use of brief quotations in a book review.

Printed in the United States of America

First Printing, 2019

ISBN: 9781694088550

NEW INTERNATIONAL VERSION® NIV® Copyright © 1973, 1978, 1984 by International Bible Society® Used by permission. All rights reserved worldwide.

ENGLISH STANDARD VERSION® Copyright© 2007, 2011, 2016 by Crossway Bibles. Used by permission. All rights reserved.

NEW KING JAMES VERSION® Copyright© 1982 by Thomas Nelson. Used by permission. All rights reserved.

Illustrator:
Marvin Eans, MFA
Graphic Design & Photography
Social Media: @marvineans
www.Eanesdc.com

Publisher:
Published by Purpose Publishing House
PurposePublishingHouse@gmail.com
www.PurposePublishingHouse.com

ABOUT THE AUTHOR

Yolanda Boone is a Speech and Language Pathologist who practices in Florida. She is a wife, a mother of three children, and, most important, an evolving woman of God. The Adventures of Abigail is her first novel.

DEDICATION

To Christ, my Lord and Savior: Thank You for being You and whispering to me throughout my childhood! You showed me how to embrace with boldness the only title that truly matters – a child of God, which is the best thing that ever happened to me. To Ms. Prewitt, my first speech and language pathologist: Thank you for introducing me to speech and language when I was five years old. Because you went above and beyond, my life is above and beyond. To my Mom, your legacy of sweetness, kindness, generosity, and creativity gifted me with a legacy to leave with the world. To my family, friends, professors, colleagues, students, intercessors, and church: Thank you for being the army that helped me to defeat the giants associated with stuttering in my life!

TABLE OF CONTENTS

FOREWORD

I met Yolanda Boone when she enrolled in Speech-Language Pathology as a graduate student at Fontbonne University, where I taught. She was a bright and motivated student, a delight to have in my class. While Yolanda was rather quiet and reserved in large groups, she expressed herself more freely in one-to-one interactions, and it was during several such meetings early during her time at Fontbonne that I saw and appreciated her wonderful sense of humor, her strong character, and the many gifts she possessed beyond her academic skills. Little did I know that she also stutters.

From what I recall, she first shared with me her history of stuttering when she enrolled in my graduate-level Fluency Disorders class. We spoke of it occasionally thereafter, though it was never the focus of our conversations. It was simply a part of her that she chose to disclose, and for that I was honored.

Yolanda and I kept in touch after she graduated from the program, and our relationship has evolved from professor-student to friendship. I treasure the times we talked on the phone or in-person over tea or lunch, and our collaborations at day-long workshops and a camp for children and teens who stutter. When Yolanda told me her dream of writing a book for young adults about stuttering, I was excited. I was privileged to read earlier drafts, which, while a work of fiction, is highly autobiographical. While reading them, Yolanda shared with me some of her early experiences with stuttering.

With Abigail, Yolanda invites you into her life and her personal journey with stuttering as a youth. If you are a person who stutters, it is important to note that your story is both very personal and different. I believe that reading about another person's perspective about stuttering may help you to think deeply about your own journey with it. At the very least, this perspective will give you a sense of comfort in knowing that you are not alone. If you are a parent, a friend, a sibling, or a speech therapist to someone who stutters, Abigail's experiences may help you to understand stuttering from the point of view of someone who lives with it in their body and soul.

I hope that this book moves you to approach the person in your life who stutters and listen to their story. Time is the greatest gift you have to give; therefore, ensure that you understand their view of stuttering, what they hope to change or not change about stuttering, and how and when they want to apply these changes. If stuttering runs in your family, you likely will have more than one story to hear! The only person who owns stuttering is the person who stutters, and in giving them the freedom to be in charge of their own speech, you give them true power and your best support.

Find a comfortable chair and immerse yourself in Abigail's wonderful adventure!

Lynne W. Shields, Ph.D. CCC-SLP
Board Certified Specialist in Fluency and Fluency Disorders
Professor Emeritus, Fontbonne University
St. Louis, Missouri

PROLOGUE: DIAMONDS

As the bus exited the parking lot of Robinhood Elementary School's Eighth Grade Center for its afternoon route, the window next to my seat became a magnet that pulled my head closer. I didn't notice my best friend Taylor waving at me to save her a seat before she plopped down on my backpack and moved to the seat behind me. She always knows when I am deep in thought and need to be left alone. The assignment I received today soured my usually exciting, stargazed, happy-camper ride home. Taylor and I usually made the journey more exciting by sharing earbuds and listening to the latest hip-hop, rap, and pop songs on her iPhone. We would also watch online videos of people doing ridiculously funny things, plot how we would convince our parents to let us spend the entire weekend together, or dream about the changes we would make to the school system. Those were our usual bus activities – all while we ignored the middle school dramatics and shenanigans that happened around us. The gossip, the craziness, and the romantics were nothing like the playful and silly elementary school bus rides. Taylor was probably reading the 500-page sci-fi novel we were supposed to read together. It is about teens who hack into cyberspace and change the world's digital clocks to borrow time from the next day to resolve a worldly problem that happened during the current day. She probably read the first 10 pages already. The teens in the book are challenged to use innovation and technology, creation, and humanity to solve a specific problem before the end of the next day. The twist is they can't use anything that was a part of the previous day's problem to fix it. The teens learn the art of thinking and creating for a better future, and not interfering with the past. I wished that this day was in the past and already!

Thursday was usually my favorite day of the week. This Thursday felt more like a sad movie in which you know the events in it will make you feel all kinds of emotions. For example, you could be crying one minute and laughing the next, and then on the edge of your seat, nervous, and angry later on. You're left wondering why people do things to cause others to feel like this, and why bad things happen to good people. Was I one of the good people? My mind drifted as I reached for the heart-shaped diamond pendant necklace that rested around my neck.

I always found myself fidgeting with the necklace when I felt uncomfortable. My grandparents bought it for my thirteenth birthday last year. It has been through some twists and turns, and a year later it's still holding up. It's not as perfect as you would expect most diamond pendant necklaces to be, but that's what made it more special to me. It has a tiny black speck in the middle that most people wouldn't notice unless they look closely or I show them. I remember how exciting it was when my Papa told me the story of how the diamond gained its significance. He reminded me of an adventurer telling a tale about an ancient discovery. It made me feel magical. I can hear his voice now.

"Abigail, when your Granny and I went shopping for your birthday, none of the gifts we contemplated buying you spoke to us like this diamond!" He sat down, leaned in close to me, lowered his voice, and spoke slow and mythical as if he were delivering a secret message. I couldn't help but become drawn into the story that followed.

"We were on our way to see *The Wiz* at The Muny in Forest Park. We left way too early and had a lot of time to kill, so your Granny insisted that we go somewhere in the area to eat, shop, and walk around. There was an echo in the wind outside of a jewelry store as we strolled down Kiener Plaza in downtown St. Louis. The day couldn't be any more beautiful. It was such a sunny day, and there was an unforgettable calmness about it. Everything was so noticeable. When you've stayed in St. Louis long enough, you'll learn that nothing is ever still or calm downtown. Loud music emanates from cars that zip by, and the drivers honk at people crossing the street. A crowd is usually arriving at or departing from concerts and events in Ballpark Village or a baseball game at Busch Stadium. But on that day, everyone appeared to be in a peaceful state as they window shopped, walked their dogs, or played in the splash pad. Other people were eating Ted Drew's Ice Cream, Imo's Pizza, fried rice, or an infamous ooey-gooey butter cake as they sat and talked or admired the view of the Gateway Arch and the Old Courthouse from benches facing the fountains on the park grounds. Again, winds were non-existent until we arrived at the storefront. I heard a whisper, and Granny and I felt and heard the nudge to enter. As we entered, the sweetest 81-year old lady greeted us. I knew she was 81 because she was wearing a Samuel Jewelry shirt that read, 'I'm 81 and still shining.' She said, 'I had a feeling a couple would come in today to shop for a very special child, so I set aside some sale items the day before.'" By then, Papa had me anxious to hear the rest of the story. He continued in a detailed play-by-play version of what happened.

"Abigail, you have to know that we did very little talking to this woman the entire time. In fact, I think I only told her you were turning thirteen. Small talk cut the air every now and then as she showed us breathtaking princess, round, and oval-cut diamonds until she brought the heart-shaped diamond. At that very moment the sun hit the store window, creating a light ray that shone on the diamond and caused the light to enter the stone. The light from that single diamond was magnified throughout the whole entry way to the store. Your Granny let out the loudest gasp of sheer amazement at its beauty. There was so much light. The lady smiled as she let us examine it closely before she warned us of the diamond's imperfection."

Papa said he tuned out the possibility of not purchasing the diamond for me and cared less about any imperfections of which the sales woman spoke. It was the words with which she left with him and Granny that turned the ultimate whisper into a loud and clear message that this diamond was meant for me. He went on to tell me what she said, "Once you get to know the imperfections of diamonds, you get to discover their radiant perfections even more." With those words, he knew they were more than just a sales pitch.

Papa then took out his magnifying glass and viewed the diamond's flaw while holding it very close to my face continuing the story. "You see, there's a carbon crystal spot that formed inside the diamond when it was born. It doesn't make the diamond less real or beautiful; it just makes it sparkle a little differently at times. It's rare, more fragile, and meant to stand out from the rest. It needed to belong to someone caring enough to appreciate its beautiful differences – which is exactly why we gave it to you." I loved when he concluded the story with a direct and loving gaze into my eyes while reciting the message engraved on the box in which the necklace came. In a low, melodic, soothing, yet powerful voice, he said, "Abigail, you were born to bring more than one kind of sparkle to the world."

The flashback reminded me why I wear the necklace every day. I desperately wanted to believe my grandfather. I believed I was pretty, smart, funny, and so much more, but I had a stuttering problem that was magnified when I was given the assignment.

CHAPTER 1

#A TEEN WITH TEENAGE FEELINGS

I could go on and on sounding like a sad song. The screeching and hissing from the bus stopping startled me. I caught a glimpse of the other kids reacting to me jerking my head up to ensure that I didn't miss my stop. "Whew!" At least the embarrassment of having to ride the entire route and circle back home wasn't one of my 99 problems for the day. It's happened to Taylor and me before. Mama must have been right when she told me that one day, I would wake up and feel like a crazy person due to puberty and hormones. She often said she hoped I stay sweet and never change. Today, I felt like crying, sleeping, eating a big tub of ice cream, and screaming all because of my annoying stutter!

I don't remember it being this big of a deal when I was younger. Back then, it was just a little bump in the road that was made smoother if I traveled at a more comfortable pace. Usually, I was fine if I concentrated on speaking a little slower and breathed a little easier. Lately, the speed bumps were everywhere, and it was hard for me to pace myself when I was the only one who was asked to drive with caution. Maybe it's the teen thing. Everything was such a big deal! The day before, a zit formed on my chin. A week ago, I had trouble finding the perfect yellow shirt. The other day, I was given a bad grade on a test. Today…"UGHHHH!" I wanted to fit in and stop looking for extra room into which to squeeze my stutter. It's just so hard trying to keep up with the other kids at school when they spoke as clearly and as fast as a Mercedes Benz, and I was the girl who trekked on a bike with training wheels. All of it made me feel like I had a dim sparkle. I wanted to pedal away from the world and leave stuttering in a mysterious hiding place.

Taylor's soft voice barely caught my attention, "Abigail, our stop is coming up." I didn't respond. I wasn't always this dramatic. The way I talked and the way I was asked to deal with it was very different from everyone else.

At school, I was asked to write about my stutter in a big, fat journal! My feelings would've been different if I had good things to say about it. Who would ask a teen to write about such a personal subject? I knew: teachers! I wasn't prepared for this. No one gave me a picture, lecture notes, an outline, fill-in-the-blank, an explicit lesson, or showed me video clips about how to do it! Who writes about *how* they speak? This was such a paradox, and it seemed like an ugly thing for me to do. If this were a movie, this would be the scene that made me feel all kinds of emotions. I've never said a curse word, but I would imagine this was the right time to say one.

CHAPTER 2

NEXT STOP, MY HAPPY PLACE: #MORE CHOCOLATE CHIP COOKIES PLEASE

The thirty-minute bus ride was over. A slight burst of wind blew our bus driver's hair out of place. By the end of our rides to and from school, you'd never know the whirlwinds Mrs. Jenkin's hair had been through because it always seemed to fall perfectly back into place. Mrs. Jenkins was only 22 years old and such a diva! The boys flirted with her, and the girls enjoyed talking to her about her fluorescent gel nails, hair color of the week, and dope graphic t-shirts. Weirdly enough, she's wearing a shirt that read "SPARKLE" today. Papa would've told me it's a sign from the man upstairs that I needed to turn my frown upside down and smile. Taylor nudged me to make sure I was paying attention. I waved at her as we departed the bus. The slight turn in her body towards me and the curious scrunch in her eyebrows as she walked in the other direction let me know she wanted to walk with me. I was glad she kept walking towards her house because I didn't feel like talking about it.

Letting go of my book bag's clammy shoulder straps from my tight clutch felt gross as I took it off at the front door of the tiny, fifty-something-year-old, sky blue, four-bedroom home on the corner of Evergreen Blvd. Granny and Papa lived there for what seemed like forever. They say the neighborhood wasn't the same as it used to be in North St. Louis county. Crime was creeping in more often these days, but Granny always said the Lord covers the house and she's not moving anywhere else. I could tell unbelievable survival stories about this house and everyone in it, but one story stands out the most. Years ago, a horrific tornado skipped over the house and ruined almost all the other homes surrounding it; therefore, I guess no one can argue with that degree of covering. I later learned that this wasn't the first time our family was protected from a tornado! When Mama was pregnant with me, a tornado touched down on the street on which she was living. She was on the phone with Granny when she heard what sounded like the loud roar of an incoming train. Granny yelled for her to step away from any windows and take cover, but she was too late. Mama watched the funnel violently spin outside of her kitchen window. It skipped over her building and made impact with the next. Since then, Granny's motto is "we're covered!"

When I exited the bus, I was surprised when I didn't see Granny standing on the porch watching the street to ward off anyone who looked like they were going to harm me. She's very protective, and she trusted no one when it came to her grandchildren. You'd think she'd be more trusting of that covering she always speaks about.

The navy blue, white, and emerald green cheerleader letterman's jacket I hung on the coat rack was damp from my sweaty armpits. I thought about kicking off my shoes at the door; however, I didn't follow through for two reasons: Granny would have a fit because one day she accidentally tripped and fell over them, and my metallic gold, high-top Converses were clowning from perspiration. I didn't need anyone adding spice to this day by making fun of my smelly feet. They didn't know what it's like to be in my shoes, literally, every day!

"Hey baby, how was school? Gotta run to the store to get some butter for your Granny to finish dinner." Before I could respond, Papa rushed passed me through the metal and glass screen door with fancy black bars on it. He's notorious for running quick errands for Granny before dinner. "Tell your mom I'll be right back," he yelled from his old black Cadillac he called 'Suzy-Q.' It's amazing how my entire family could squeeze and sandwich our way into his car.

I thought I was going to have the table to myself for a while. I opened the journal in which I'm expected to write my first entry by next Thursday, but nothing more than thoughts about my diamond necklace, sad movies, moving far away from stuttering, and all sorts of feelings came to mind. I was so lost. I wished that Ms. Plewitt stopped to think about how the assignment would've made me feel. I was supposed to be in a happy place.

The fresh-baked chocolate chip cookies my mama left on the table had me thinking about her. She's nothing short of amazing. I always heard her tell her friends that I was the one she could count on to make her smile after a hard day of work, help her around the house, and warm her heart with Eskimo kisses. She even told me stories about how the stars were so bright the night before I was born. She thought she could see constellations. The way she told the story was she knew that the stars were a sign of how bright I would shine one day. Just the thought of her voice made me smile.

"There's my girl," she said leaning into my nose to sneak in a quick Eskimo kiss. "Mom! I'm getting too old for that." A laugh erupted, despite my efforts to hold it in as she quickly snuck in another one.

"Let me know if you need help with your homework. I have to work tonight, so I'll be turning it in for a nap soon."

"Yes ma'am," I replied. "A-a-actually, I-I got this assignment from Ms. Plewitt that I-I..."

"Oh, it's so nice to know you get to work with her again this year. I really like her. Did she give you a daily challenge calendar this year? That calendar really got you speaking up more over the years. I need to call her to let her know about all the speaking challenges you completed this summer. When you told the waitress at that Italian restaurant you stutter and might need a little extra time to speak when you order your food, I was so proud of you. That took so much courage! She even stopped me to tell me she was so impressed, and she knew nothing about stuttering beforehand."

"Yeah, and she gave us free gluten-free molten chocolate lava c-cake that day too," I said as I tried to ignore the fact that she interrupted me. I reminisced with her. Chocolate had its way of making me forgive and forget everything, including mama's frequent interruptions. About three cookies later, she was still talking about it. She brought up of some of the most embarrassing moments of my history with stuttering that I gravely wanted to forget. The struggle was very real, and I couldn't lie about how challenging speaking was at times. I used to have her order my food at restaurants and speak to the doctors on my behalf during checkups. I would also drop the first part of my name and tell people that my name was Gail in order to not stutter on the 'A'. I have a hard time saying "Hello" when the phone rings, so I found myself dropping the 'H' and saying "ello" just to get it out after a long pause. Usually, the memories would've upset me, but I continued eating the cookies. The taste of the sweet chocolate morsels that melted in my mouth drowned her voice out. It made me think of how far I'd come before my thought was interrupted with, "I wonder if your IEP meeting to discuss your progress in speech therapy is coming up soon?"

"I-I don't know," was all I could say. The last thing I was worried about was an Individualized Education Program (IEP) meeting with Ms. Plewitt to talk more about my stutter. My eyes wandered down to the necklace as I started to find some comfort in holding it. I reminded myself that it was a very special gift and it had me as its owner. It was in the hands of someone who wanted it, regardless of its differences. I loved my diamond necklace to pieces. My mom and grandparents must've felt that way about me. Maybe I should've tried to feel the same way about my stutter. I placed my hand over the necklace and felt my heart beginning to beat at a calmer rhythm, and took a slow, deep breath. Somehow that helped me to remember I can try to make the best of journaling my stutter.

CHAPTER 3

#READY, SET, JUST KIDDING!

A jam-packed kitchen was moments away, so I scribbled some thoughts in the journal before everyone came home from their after-school activities.

~~Dear Journal~~

Dear Ms. Plewitt,

Why? Why? Why do I have to do this?

Can we just talk about my speech instead?

You know what stuttering is so just tell me how to be done with this already!

Eventually, doodles filled the page. Normally this would be okay, but not for this journal. Rubber eraser bits and pencil smears made their way onto the paper before I was carried away with some sort of cartoon or life-like drawing of a better moment than this one. It made me think of the sentences I used to write to go along with the pictures that describe how I felt about stuttering in Ms. Plewitt's class when I was younger.

Stuttering is breakdancing with words.

Stuttering is a computer taking forever to load.

Stuttering is a pain in the you know what!

Stuttering is interrupting yourself over and over.

Stuttering is like hiccups. After a million years no one knows a cure, but there are a few things you can do to help it go away! The problem is it comes back when you least expect it sometimes.

Stuttering is speed bumps, pebbles, rocks, potholes, and cracks in the road. You must be careful to avoid them, but if you hit one don't panic. The road will eventually smooth out again.

It was clear that I had nothing good to say about stuttering. Holding the notebook inches away from my face, out of frustration I ripped the page of scribbles to confetti. A few thoughts made their way to the second page before I had to rebel from writing anything else. "Just close the book," I told myself. I cleared the table of all my textbooks, Number 2 pencils, erasers, and the journal in one sweep into my book bag before making a peaceful exit to my room for some privacy. I hoped to figure out a way to make this a little more exciting later.

Ms. Plewitt,

Stuttering isn't what most people probably think it is.

CHAPTER 4

MR. BEE'S HIVE: #BEEHIVE, #STYLE, #OUCH

A roar of laughter filled the school when our principal, Mr. Bee, started morning announcements with, "Welcome, fellow Dragons, on this gorgeous Friday in the hood!" Our school was far from resembling anything in the hood. He continued with a loud, "Give yourself and your shoulder partners a fired up congrats for making it a great first week of school. Let's remember to tame our inner dragon today, so the slayers don't have to come out to play." Another one of Mr. Bee's corny catchphrases he threw in every day. I knew he's always trying to teach us about humor and figurative speech in the seventh and eighth-grade wings of the school. That day, I wasn't laughing. Our school didn't relate much to medieval times, Robinhood, or dragons. Our dragon is a statue that breathed a flame of robots, books, computers, mathematical symbols, a microphone, and a ballerina on the front lawn of our campus. Last summer, all the teachers and the student body came together to sculpt it. We had a pep rally dedicated to hyping our school's new values and core beliefs, and to encourage students to commit to exploring and developing their inner scientist, artist, technologist, and mathematician. Everyone bought into the school being the first elementary/ middle school with a science, technology, engineering, performing arts, mathematics, and robotics program built into the curriculum. What I didn't expect was every teacher making *everything* about it. The more serious side of Mr. Bee always said science is in everything, and he's on a quest to help every student master the science of every subject. All the teachers worked hard to show him they're a perfect fit in his colony. We might as well had been home of the Bees!

On Monday, he gave each teacher a stack of student interests, learning style, and multiple intelligences questionnaires for the students to complete. They read, "Go the extra mile. Know your style!" They're supposed to give the teachers an understanding of our learning style and which activities would help us master the skills the state of Missouri wanted us to know. We were also told they will help us to own our learning experiences.

Every morning, Mr. Bee also quoted from Greek philosophers such as Socrates during his announcements. He'd say, "Know thyself" and add "to further thyself." So, I guess the questionnaires were his way of making that happen. He really dedicated himself to turning all of us into distinguished worker bees to find our own style to get ahead in school and in life.

On Wednesday morning, my homeroom teacher returned my questionnaire with a smile and a comment that read "You've got a lot of style!" written in bright magenta pink. Check boxes were selected for the highest scores in learning by hearing and seeing things, nature, art, creating, writing, Geography, and Science. At the bottom of the page, my multiple areas of intelligence were categorized in those big ole' words that I didn't quite understand. The description on the back read that Intrapersonal means something about being connected to how I feel, my abilities, and self-reflection. I had no clue how that applied to me, but I could relate to the Verbal-Linguistic category, which means being able to use words effectively for reading, writing, listening, and speaking. I disagreed with the speaking part when I stuttered, but words have always been fascinating to me. I think you can do some powerful things with them on paper.

The whole questionnaire was freakishly right about all my strengths and interests, except for Geography. I couldn't tell the difference between north and south if I was riding down the street from my house! I loved Social Studies, History, and learning about the cultures of different countries around the world.

The problem with the questionnaire was Ms. Plewitt took advantage of it to give me the monumental project of journaling about my stutter! She usually gave me homework that she would have no way of knowing when or how I did it! This year, she switched things up in the hive, and I didn't know if I was going to get used to the taste of this season's honey. Ouch! What a sting!

CHAPTER 5

#READY, AIM...

Hammering school bells opened the floodgates to the perfect middle school mixer in the hallways between classes. Air high-fives, head nods, and fist bumps from fellow cheerleaders and some kids in my classes briefly took my mind off my drama. Pushing through cliques, couples, athletes, and band members who carried huge instruments while I avoided violators of the No Texting and Walking rule made getting to each class on time a nightmare. I learned that if I make eye contact with someone long enough, they would start a conversation with me and make me late. For that reason, I made it a point to look down every now and then.

A pair of cute, funky, chunky, brown wedge sandal heels appeared within a few feet of me before they stopped. I hoped it's not who I thought it was! My eyes traveled upwards to a long, flowy, earth-toned, forest green maxi dress cinched at the waist with a vintage, rustic, brown leather belt. A bold emerald and gold arrow on a droopy necklace with earrings accessorized the free-spirited teacher with which I'm all too familiar.

Her red, candy-colored painted lips and perfectly made-up cat eyes looked directly at me, confirming my biggest fear. Dang! It's her. Ms. Plewitt!

"Hey Abigail. I hope you have a good weekend."

"Thanks, y-you too," I said while anticipating her next dreaded topic of conversation.

To my surprise, she continued walking and didn't mention the journal. The rear view of her neat bohemian goddess braid had me thanking God she was gone!

Ms. Plewitt was my Speech teacher since the first grade. Oops! I did it again! She hated when others called her that! The correct title is Speech and Language Pathologist (SLP).

Anyway, she's been my Speech and Language Pathologist for a long time. Normally, I'd brag about how wonderful she was, compliment her medieval bohemian-like outfits, or follow her to her classroom to get out of my regular classes, but that day I didn't! She became the boho chick who flipped my week upside down, turned it around, and struck me to the ground with her fancy medieval bow with an arrow of a stupid journal assignment about stuttering. Why'd you have to do me like that Ms. Plewitt? Why'd you have to make me your target?

To clarify, she didn't literally strike me. I felt like she did because I was forced to do an assignment that I didn't want to do, which was probably more painful than being in the line of fire of an angry dragon. I had only one expected outcome!

CHAPTER 6

#FIRE!

I 'd be lying if I said I purposely gave the journal any more thought the rest of the school day.

I had the hardest time hiding the biggest and cheesiest grin as I hurried to get to my last period Creative Performing Arts elective class. We're beginning the school year with poetry, and I couldn't wait to dive in and show off my rhyming skills. I was already feeling good about getting an A in the class. Suddenly, the thought of Ms. Plewitt's arrow being thrust into my chest and a big, fat, bleeding, red "F" on my journaling assignment crossed my mind as I spotted her walking towards me again! Here comes the dragon. I was about to be burned to a crisp. How in the world did she walk back to this end of the hall in those clunky shoes so fast? She was just going in the opposite direction! I did a 180-degree spin looking for a way out of her sight. A hiding place was nowhere to be found; no nearby bathrooms in which to run, no friends to hide behind at their lockers, no drinking fountains to stoop in front of, and no signs telling her to hold her horses and make a U-turn.

I needed to be rescued and swept away by an imaginary knight in shining armor who rode a stallion with a silver chaffron metal cover over its face to protect me from Ms. Plewitt. The click-clack from her heels were about five feet away. My eyes grew big and sweat dripped down my armpits. "Hi again Abigail," she said in her classic happy-go-lucky voice. I waved and nervously smiled as she uttered the dreaded question of" How is the journal coming?"

I gulped as if I swallowed a frog.

Before I could answer, she continued, "Take your time this weekend and next week. Write whatever comes to mind. Go where your pen takes you."

I was saved when the blare of the bell cut the conversation short!

"Well, I have to run. See ya' next week," she said.

I waved and left her with a stuttered, "O-Okay." Once again, she kept the same peppy smile and went on her way. I wish my pen would take me to a kingdom far, far away like when Shrek set out to rescue Princess Fiona. I didn't know who was going to rescue Princess Abigail from this treacherous assignment.

CHAPTER 7

#MS. SCOTT: CREATIVE PERFORMING ARTS

"Alright class," yelled Ms. Scott before she eventually whispered, "In five, four, three, two – how are you?"

"Ready!" (clap) "To do!" (clap, clap) "What-we- came- here-to-do! (clap, clap, clap)," we chanted and clapped in a double-dutch, nursery rhyme, down- down baby, knick-knack-paddy-whack type of beat in response to her attention getter for the class. Her whisper always seemed to shut everyone up quicker than a yelling and repeated clapping match with us. It's like she knew the only way we could hear her whisper was to tune in completely to what she's saying. We must face her and really watch her in order to respond correctly. She's tried to trip us up several times by whispering some off-the-wall comments.

Ms. Scott didn't waste any time getting straight to her plans for the day.

"Since it's the first week of class, we have to set learning goals and present them in your focus groups." Hands immediately shot up.

"Yes, TJ?" she asked.

"What are focus groups again?" he asked while he looked around to see who else had their hand up.

I guess the others had the same question because their hands fell down just as quickly as they went up.

Ms. Scott's perfect pearly whites commanded our attention as she explained, "Focus groups are intended to pair a good mix of students together to teach you the life skill of learning to work with anyone and everyone, no matter how similar or different you are."

Heads sprung up like chickens to pay close attention as she continued, "Mr. Bee's reasoning behind this is to create balance. As a group, we are to learn and use each other's strengths, weaknesses, and gifts to increase the success of the group as a whole. You can't achieve success without balance and learning to trust others, help others, and communicate with others is the only way to get there."

Her tired, hosed, bare feet circled the room while she read all of us with her eyes before she moved on.

"Any questions? Yes, TJ?"

"So, we're basically responsible for each other in this class?"

The Adventures of Abigail

"Yes, yes, yes. Precisely!" she confirmed.

Her cheeks must've hurt from smiling so much, I thought.

"YESSSSSSS! I don't have to do all the work by myself!" TJ belted out.

"Easy A!" I heard someone else blurt out.

"Actually, this might be the hardest A you've ever worked for in your young 13 or 14 years of life. Fifteen for those of you we are welcoming to the class to fulfill the requirements of the curriculum," she responded as she slowly walked around the room and tapped her tie-dye-patterned pointer stick in one hand. She continued. "Working to achieve a goal with others in mind besides yourself is a difficult skill to master. It changes everything. If one person in the group is falling or not getting to equally shine, then the group has to figure out a way to use everything they know about one another to make sure everyone is successful."

"Imani?" she called in response to seeing Imani's hand dart up.

"So, you can't just do it for them or speak for them or whatever?"

"Absolutely NOT!" Ms. Scott responded with an amused giggle in her voice.

"Everyone has to learn and believe that we all are fully capable of doing everything we put our minds to. There are no limitations. We just have to use our strengths and know it's perfectly okay to be creative and express things in different ways."

Ms. Scott switched to a friendlier but very serious tone and exclaimed, "Creativity is a unique gift we've all been given as individuals from the time we were created!"

"In life you will learn that it is your very own creative blueprint that only you possess in your genetic makeup that will allow you the ability to somehow relate to and help others. You just have to be willing to navigate through your blueprint – get to know it. And even better – listen to it and follow it. And if you think creativity is only arts and crafts, then I am SO happy you are in my class!"

Mr. Bee had her trapped in the hive, too! This was her quest to teach us the science of creativity.

Confusion and curiosity seemed to mask all our faces. Ms. Scott could be so deep with her lessons that it sometimes took deep sea snorkeling gear to bring her back to shallow water. Luckily, our faces were all the gear we needed to bring her back to the surface.

"In other words," she paused, "you have to be brave to be creative. You have to be willing to explore and find adventure in areas you wouldn't normally say are the strongest things about you. It will be fun, yet scary, and challenging at times, but don't be afraid. That's what learning is about. And the things you will discover about yourself, in the end, are priceless!"

Now I knew why a perfectly written cursive message and essential questions were written on the board.

Creativity is your adventure!

What might you discover along the way? Will you go far enough? Will you climb high enough? Will you discover hidden treasures?

"Now, shall we begin to create, class?

Most of us still looked like deer in headlights. Some of us seemed to nod before she belted out, "One, two!"

"Let's do it. Let's do (clap) what we came here to do (clap, clap, clap)!" Our chant wasn't as thrilling as the first one. Most of us sounded like cheerleaders at the end of a cold soccer game in which the Dragons were losing.

I was excited about all of this. Poetry was becoming my thing, so I thought it would be a piece of cake! But what in the world did she mean by everyone shining and finding hidden treasures? That's a little too deep for me to understand. I thought about asking her what she meant, but I didn't want to stutter or sound like I didn't know what was going on. All I thought about was what was written on the board as she continued talking.

"Creativity is your adventure!" Creativity with words is something to which I know I can relate.

CHAPTER 8

#FOCUS

"Now class, let's start forming the foundation to your success in this class—your focus groups. Your groups have been preselected based on the learning profiles and questionnaires you did earlier this week in homeroom. Go to your assigned stations and follow the directions in the folder on each round table."

Coach, Supporter, Cheerleader, Referee, and Secretary were the roles from which we had to choose. I mistakenly chose to be the secretary because I thought all I had to do was take notes and keep a record of the group's plans. I was bamboozled! This year, the secretary must present a summary of the notes at the end of each focus group meeting. I almost excused myself to the bathroom so I wouldn't have to present anything. Ms. Plewitt made it very clear to me that avoiding talking in class was a big no-no, and it would only make me feel worse.

As a sidebar, I didn't agree. Three years ago, in fifth grade, I had a teacher who was new to the school, and I guess no one had the chance to tell Ms. Thompson that I stuttered. One day, she called on me to read aloud in class and my words took about 10 seconds too long to escape my lips. I paused between words, I couldn't form the beginning of sentences, and I repeated words over and over. It was a mess. Ms. Thompson told me to hurry up and insisted that I was acting like I didn't want to read. The other kids in my class began laughing at me. She told me she knew I was a good reader and threatened to call my mama If I didn't read the next paragraph well. Her definition of 'well' was fast enough for the next student to continue reading the rest of the story before the bell rang. When I came home from school, I cried so hard that my mama called the school and used curse words I didn't even know existed. After that conversation, Miss Thompson gave me candy, let me help grade spelling tests, and even gave me gifts for Christmas, Valentine's Day, and my birthday. Even though the queen-like royal treatment was nice, nothing she did could ever erase the feeling of the embarrassment she caused me. That was probably the day I started to hate reading and speaking in front of the class. I panicked every time I thought someone was going to call on me because I remember that day so well. I never want to feel like that again.

You would think I'd chicken out and not do my part in the group that day. As much as my mind was telling me not to try, I did it anyway only because I didn't want my team to think I was afraid of talking altogether. I liked to talk! I just don't like stuttering in front of my classmates. "Maybe it'll be a smooth speech day," I thought. Here goes.

CHAPTER 9

SOS! #SAVE OUR STUTTERER #TEEN IN DISTRESS

As I presented the notes about the team name we created, the roles we chose, the rules for being a good teammate, and the calendar of upcoming assignments, my stutter peeked outside of the curtain and reared its ugly head. During the daunting final project of reciting poetry at the Fall Performing Arts Show, my stutter began to steal the show. It performed set after set, monologue after monologue, line after line, and stutter after stutter. I couldn't focus on anything else. My necklace was starting to feel more like a fidget spinner in my fingers.

Everyone in my group stared at me the entire time. I couldn't help but wonder what thoughts were going through all their heads. I thought I was paired with some nice kids who probably would never tease or bully me for stuttering, but I didn't know enough about them to be sure. I only know of them from word of mouth and some good things I've noticed about them at school over the years. Sadly, it still didn't stop me from stuttering.

Imani Z. was one of the dance team captains and a fashionista who took her school work very seriously to stay on the team. She's from West Africa. She wore the most intricate, colorful, and gorgeous clothes when she wasn't in uniform. The bold crimson reds, the royal blues; the golden safari yellows and browns; the tiger oranges; the forest, jade, and lime greens; and the grape hues of violet always caught my attention. I often wondered if she imported her skirts and dresses directly from her birthplace. I couldn't find anything like it in the local malls. Her accent and matchless talent in singing were just as beautiful. At last year's Spring Performance Arts Show, she sang an opera song that had a spiritual, holy-like effect on the audience. Most students, including myself, didn't know the language in which she sang it, but so many of us cried because her voice was very alluring. Teachers were bawling.

She chose to be the cheerleader in the group. She did nothing of the sort! I thought, "Cheer me on Imani! Tell me how great it is that I'm even trying to continue through the whole presentation. Congratulate me on being brave and not quitting because of the stuttering. Isn't the definition of a cheerleader in this situation someone who should cheer me on as I lead this presentation, or someone who made me more cheerful as I lead? Tell me it was a great accomplishment! Better yet, tell me to go and fight so that I can win!"

Lauryn B. chose to be the team supporter. She also did nothing! Lauryn was always so kind, and her smile was contagious. Her smile alone could solve all the school's problems. Last year, she ran for student council president and passed out buttons with her big smile on it. I thought it was cool watching a wave of smiles form across everyone's face as soon as they looked at it. I'm sure she won by popular demand by virtue of the personality that came with her smile. I could tell people wanted to be around her. She was their happy medium or safe place or something, and I wanted her to be the same for me.

"Lauryn, where is your support? You're killing me softly! Tell everyone that staring isn't nice! Encourage everyone to look down at the paper while I read. Use your smile to fix it all. Do something, girl!" I thought.

Zack S. chose to be the coach.

He was the quiet mathematician in the group who probably believed in solving every problem in the world with an algorithm. It's great that he's the coach because he seemed to get everything right all the time. He always took his time to respond to questions and hated when people interrupted his thinking. I'd trust him with anything! His grandparents were from India, and every Christmas break he traveled with them. They were raising him for reasons unknown. He didn't look like he had much Indian in him, especially with his bright blue eyes and blonde hair. I guess his hair could've been dyed. He was a big help to Taylor and me at summer camp in June when we completed a project on the history and culture of India. Supposedly, he's really into computers and technology, too – which weren't my forte'! He often looked sad, but with his smarts I couldn't figure out why.

He also did absolutely nothing but stare! I couldn't help but to stare back in hopes that my eyes would signal the following information: "Come on, coach! Tell me what to do next! Coaching isn't a spectator sport! Do I need to steal a megaphone from the athletic department? Wait – maybe that's the referee's job. Anyhow, tell the rest of the team how to respond in a situation like this, play by play."

TJ chose to be our referee. At first, I thought this role might be too serious for him. I could only picture him blowing a whistle or interceding to make us crack up laughing. He's the class clown, but he somehow made difficult tasks fun. At times he may need a minute to get focused, but I guess that's why he had us in the group. TJ also saw Ms. Plewitt because he talked a mile a minute and needed help with vocabulary. Two years ago, we were in the same speech group and I learned a plethora of words just by listening to Ms. Plewitt work with him. He mentioned to her that his visits helped his rap game so that he could spit tighter bars in his flows. He also played the drums in the school's band and…his perfectly straight teeth and dimples could put permanent creases in my cheeks!

The referee gave me nothing! He didn't even interrupt the moment, so I thought to telepathically speak to him, "Focus TJ! Call a foul! Call a timeout to give me time to smooth out my bumpy speech."

When I fumbled through the last sentence, I tried to avoid watching everyone watch me. I looked over at Taylor in hopes that Ms. Scott needed me to join her group because of odd numbers or something. I wasn't so lucky. She appeared to be reviewing notes with her focus group in the same secretarial role as I. She looks so confident. I may be more comfortable talking in front of everyone and just as confident if she were in my group.

When I looked back at my group, they were still silent. What in the world is happening to me today? I can't even report a short summary to our group without stuttering. And as TJ would probably say, I can't do it without chopping, screwing, and making the words drop to a stuttered beat. I can't slow it down then speed it up, bring it together, and then pan the beat. The more I stuttered, the more my mind wandered to my journal. I somewhat need it right now to let out my frustrations about this unwanted beat down I just got from a rap battle I lost between the stuttered lyrics and bars I couldn't spit out of my mouth today.

"Are you okay Abigail?" Imani asked.

"Yep," I said to avoid any further discussions about it.

They should've known I wasn't okay. Who is okay with not speaking when and how they want? Not me!

Blank faces and mannequin-like bodies filled the group's spaces. My group clearly didn't know how to respond to all my stuttering. Neither did I.

Tick, tock, tick tock, the bell rang.

Finally! The school bell became the referee's whistle our group was missing to initiate my rescue from being tackled by stutters.

CHAPTER 10

#WAKE UP

The bumpy bus ride threw my pencil onto the floor and probably all the way to the front, forcing me to stop journaling. I even tried to sleep during the remainder of the ride home and wished that I could wake up to learn all of this is just a dream. Nothing made me feel any better. The roaring diesel engine, rattling windows, shaky seats, screeching halts, sharp turns, bouncing bodies, and wobbling heads from the jacked-up, cracked-up pavement and potholes were enough to keep me wide awake and stuck in this moment.

What was Ms. Plewitt going to do with the information about today's catastrophe in my journal?

"Are you starting Ms. Scott's first poetry assignment in that notebook already? You're such a nerd," Taylor teased.

I started to just go with it and tell her "yes," but I also felt safe enough to be straight up with her.

"I wish I could say that's what I was working on. C-C-Can you believe, Ms. Plewitt, my Speech and Language Pathologist (SLP), a-asked me to start journaling about how I feel about my stutter? I'm c-convinced that she's lost her mind. I just started it this week and I-I-I really don't want to do it."

I could hear crickets between us after I shared that information with her. I knew she wasn't puzzled or anything. Taylor knew my stutter very well. She's probably thinking of how to put her Positive Patty, Mother Teresa, optimistic spin on her answer – like she always did. I fished for her comforting words.

"I definitely want to read it when you are finished, if that's okay. I mean, to me – it must be kind of hard to be so nice and smart, have such great things to say, AND stutter. I hope that doesn't sound mean. It's just that – sometime I want to ask you about it, but then I don't because it doesn't even matter to me that you stutter."

If only the world thought like Taylor! I kept listening.

"Even though you don't want to do it now, I bet it will help you be more confident or something. Or it could make you feel better about it. Maybe you should find a way to make writing about it fun, like a comic strip since you are good at drawing. Or short, creative stories like the time we wrote and published stories in the Creative Enrichment

Program." Taylor snorted as she burst out laughing and continued teasing me, "You wrote soooo many stories and got mad because the teacher wouldn't read them all."

"Yeah that was k-kinda funny. I-It's not the same with this," I responded.

"You could also do poetry or something. Just be yourself. Just start writing. Write what you know you know," she suggested.

Taylor will surely be the cause of changing something in the world for the betterment of humanity or something one day. She is the only person who managed to get me to smile and see things a little differently today. Her blue-trimmed glasses slid down her skinny nose as she buried them into the book we finally started reading together for the rest of the ride home. Blue was Taylor's favorite color to compliment her tomboyish athletic wardrobe. She's the only girl I know who owns about 20 hoodies and sweatshirts with matching Jordan shoes to pair with her predicted skinny jeans. We were such opposites when it came to fashion. Girly-girl, glitter, and rose pink should've been my middle names. If I mixed the colors of fashionable Converse high top sneakers to match all my outfits, I was good. Fashion design was my goal in life. It's too bad that I couldn't dress or design my way out of this part.

CHAPTER 11

I SURRENDER!

Taylor gave me food for thought. Ms. Plewitt could come up with some pretty cool ideas and lessons, but I still couldn't find anything neat about that one! I would've appreciated it if she gave me a choice in the matter. It's not that I would've said, "no" or anything, but I wanted to choose how to do it. She told me to write whatever I wanted in the journal to capture how I felt when I stutter and what happened around me. Taylor also had me thinking about her wanting to ask me about my stutter. What would I tell Taylor if she asked me about it? What would I tell my focus group if they asked? So far, Ms. Plewitt was the only person who asked me how I felt about my stutter. That made me think no one else wanted to hear about it, so I never talked about it. Ms. Plewitt, you can thank Taylor for that one. I surrendered!

As a side bar, in no way did I plan for the journal to be an ordinary Dear Diary journal. If I was going to do it, it had to be done my way for me to truly illustrate how I felt about stuttering. As my math teacher said, "Don't tell me anything! We're from the show me state, so you must show me everything."

I sighed as I exhaled, and I found myself twirling my necklace between my thumb and index finger. I thought, "Are you ready for this show, Ms. Plewitt?" I couldn't wait to get home.

43

CHAPTER 12

#MR. BEE'S COLLABORATION 101

This is What Happens When Ms. Plewitt and Ms. Scott Come Together!

"Whew! I made it to Friday!" It felt good to sit down. I sank in the worn armchair at the long, old, wooden dining table hidden in the back of the teacher's professional learning lab. I had such a busy day. I thought I saw about 20 kids today on top of three IEP meetings. I also had to go home and write a report. My day never ended as an SLP. A forty-five-minute routine Friday teacher's meeting was 44 long minutes away from ending, according to the digital clock on the wall that's already set five minutes slow.

"Ms. Scott," I whispered.

"Psssst. Psssst. Hey, Ms. Scott, come sit by me," my voice carried before I got her full attention.

Ms. Scott rolled her eyes at the annoyed jeers from some of the uptight teachers in the room. The after-school data team meeting hadn't even fully started.

"Ahem," Mr. Bee cleared his throat to signal for Ms. Scott to sit down before he started the first item on his agenda. Luckily, he played some loud video clips on Teacherz Tubez of teachers teaching sample lessons and let us discuss them with our shoulder partners.

"Hey girl, it's good to see you," said Ms. Scott.

"Good to see you, too. How are things going this week? You look a little stressed," Ms. Scott commented.

"I am. I know we're not supposed to discuss students outside of IEP meetings, but I am just worried that I may have made a mistake in giving Abigail the journal assignment. I didn't even formally ask her if she wanted to do it. I just wonder how she's coming along with it. I bumped into her a couple times and she looked so tense – like she was afraid of me or mad at something I did."

"Ms. Plewitt, first of all, do we ever really ask our students if they want to do our assignments?"

"You know it's different in Speech and Language Therapy. It's my job to give students activities they enjoy and can relate to so they really learn how to use the skills outside of therapy," I replied.

"Sounds like my job too," Ms. Scott laughed. "Now you know she is going to do very well! You've been the best SLP for her since she was a baby here at Robinhood. She trusts you and won't let you down. And you know she is so creative. That's one of the reasons I'm so glad we met to discuss her learning style inventory. I mean, how perfect do you think a journal would be for a student like her? Her writing skills are good and need to keep being developed with creative assignments like this one. I remember when she was in the first grade. She won the 'I Love my Mom Because' essay contest. Oh, and I am so happy she met the state's criteria to participate in the school's Gifted and Creative Enrichment Program for creatively talented students. It is phenomenal that they're bringing the program into the classrooms this year, so the whole class benefits. The entire school has come up with some ingenious activities to use in our instruction. We've learned to engage all our students and seize the moments of creativity that happen because of it.

I used to just redirect students back to exactly what I was teaching from my lesson plan when they veered off, but now they are the directors. There aren't too many dull moments in my classroom anymore. Not to brag, but I've even scored Distinguished and Innovating on my teacher evaluations two years in a row simply because I've changed my way of thinking. Abigail and all our students can't turn their gifts off and on from classroom to classroom. That is precisely why we all have to nurture Abigail's talent, or she will miss out on several learning opportunities and stop believing in her creative abilities! You had best believe she will probably surprise you with a product you never expected. Like everything else, she will find creativity in this assignment too!"

Mrs. Scott is always long winded, so I had to jump in the conversation somewhere.

"I only hope I am continuing to be the best SLP for her. She's growing up. She's maturing. I bet she's starting to notice all sorts of things she never knew existed in the world of stuttering. It's not like I can play the same old Go Fish, Head Bandz, Story Cube, or Taboo board games with her to practice using smooth speech all the time. I'm sure she's starting to really think about how it makes her feel."

"Exactly! That's why she needs the journal right now. It might even compliment the poetry unit we are doing in my Creative Performing Arts elective this semester."

"Okay teachers. At this point in our data team meetings we are going to break off into your teams to discuss specific students or upcoming projects and assignments you will be working on. Remember to Bee collaborative and include everyone in the hive. That means Art, Music, PE, Occupational Therapy, Creative Arts, Physical Therapy, Math, English, Science, Social Studies, and Speech Therapy," Mr. Bee announced just as he looked at me.

Ms. Scott and I continued our discussion while we joined the group of eighth grade PE, English, and Social Studies teachers. My buddy, Mrs. Schivers, the Occupational Therapist spotted me and ran over to our table. We must have been popular that day because Mrs. Smith, the Art teacher, joined us as well. Quick and loud chatter began to drown out our conversation.

"Well, Mr. Bee's quest for all of us teachers to discover and master the science of all of our students is different when it comes to treating fluency disorders in Speech Therapy. There are so many layers to treating stuttering, and it starts with far more than what you see and hear. It's personal, it's cognitive, it's emotional, it's the five senses, it's listening beyond the messages, and it's imaginative. It's more of a language than a science to master. And the language comes in waves. At first it seems foreign, harsh, and unforgiving, but the longer you study the waves the more in tune you become to its language. It is then when the waves get stirred up, hit riptides, and high tides that you master how to endure the process leading to the calm. Learning the language of each individual person who stutters is every SLP's calm. It's being willing to go off the deep end for these kids and letting your feet touch the ocean floor a few times."

Ms. Scott reassured me with a gentle and affirming nod. "Now you're speaking my language."

"I'm just trying to learn to slow down enough to speak the language of this wave of Abigail's life. How can I help her emotionally and not just physically with her stuttering right now? How can I teach her to accept it? It's hard."

"Sounds like you need to hear that IT'S BELIEVING too," interrupted Mrs. Schivers. She's my prayer warrior here at Robinhood.

"You're right. I have to trust the tools God has given me and be guided by the spirit. And that holy grail stack of textbooks on treating fluency disorders I've collected over the years."

"Yes. Amen. And pray for Abigail to be guided by the spirit as well. Kids are never too young for that. After all, that's the most powerful tool for all of us," concluded Mrs. Schivers before her cell phone scared the life out of everyone. Before Mr. Bee could say anything, an echoed "Hello!" between the doorway and the hall trailed behind her as she answered the call.

Mrs. Schivers advice stuck with me. Until this very moment I don't think I ever realized I've been guilty of trying to be the guide, steering the wheel, and controlling the waves. What would happen if I let go? What if I allowed the waves to drift me to the shore and follow God's footsteps in the sand? Would Mr. Bee let me go with the flow and swim with the riptides in my therapy program? He can't possibly expect me to try to do things exactly like the classroom teachers!

I zoned out for a moment.

Now it's all clicking for me. This is what I do for a living! If I want to really learn Abigail's language of how she stutters, when she stutters, how it makes her feel, and help her control it, then I must think about how we all learn language in the first place. I must learn to just listen to her. I have to learn to read her. Reading is the foundation of language! It is only then when I can truly teach her to enjoy the language in which she's swimming. I want to teach her how to slow down in an ocean crowded with other sometimes stronger and faster swimmers. I want to teach her to float a bit, tread water, catch the waves, and read the water she's in to spot the breaking waves of riptides and handle them. I want her to allow the water to drift her into opportunities to surf, splash, and play a bit – opportunities to jump in time and time again to become the strongest swimmer she can be no matter her surroundings.

"I just want her to enjoy talking and be the best communicator she can be!"

"There you go, you got this!" Ms. Scott reassured.

"Mr. Bee is good for making us therapists feel like a classroom teacher. I'm just hoping and praying he doesn't ask me for a detailed explicit lesson plan on how I'm going to apply waves, riptides, footsteps, and speech to the state learning standards, use ongoing assessment to evaluate her progress, create a rubric, and all that classroom teacher jazz."

"Tell me about it! My poetry unit of study is like a book! It took me two weeks to complete it! Although, it's going to be worth it at the performing arts show this year. Just wait and see! And by the way, I wrote you and I would be working together to help every student be able to express themselves through poetry in my lesson plan. Abigail and TJ might be asked to perform in front of the school at the show with their group."

"What?"

"No pressure. That's why we're collaborating," Ms. Scott looked at me with pleading eyes. "We can't place any limitations on them. We're going to help them both through this wave. Together."

"It's not that I'm underestimating her or TJ, but I know for a fact Abigail doesn't enjoy reading out loud in class, so how do we go from that extreme to the next? That's like asking a kid to go from singing in the mirror to performing in front of a sold-out stadium. It's not that she wouldn't do it, but it's important to consider *how she* wants to be a part of the show and not force her to be front and center.

Mrs. Schivers returned at the tail end of our conversation. "You know it will probably just take God to put that desire in her heart. She's obviously got some skills. You know what they say, 'show me the area where you struggle and God will show you where he wants to use you.' That's when He really decides to put on a show. I bet God wants to use Abigail to show all of us a little something. And there's no doubt He's going to use you, too. Get ready! I bet He wants to show up and show out!"

Ms. Scott made me eat my own words quick, fast, and in a hurry! "Look at it as one of those opportunities for her to jump in you spoke about. Let her splash and play a bit. Let her feel the process of becoming a stronger communicator."

Mr. Bee must have heard Mrs. Schivers mention the word 'show' as he circled the room to check with every group. "Miss Schivers and Ms. Plewitt, I think it's fantastic you are volunteering to assist Ms. Scott with this year's performing arts show. My wife, I mean our music teacher, Mrs. Bee, was just telling me she needed some fresh and innovative ideas this year. This is great! I'm sure you have something special in your tool boxes! You can get with her group at next week's meeting."

"Certainly Mr. Bee," I muttered.

Helping Ms. Scott wasn't an issue at all. Abigail was my focus. I rarely noticed her stutter in my class anymore, so stepping out into Ms. Scott's regular classroom would give me a better picture of how she communicates in other settings. Part of me thought she might've been ready to graduate from Speech Therapy at the end of the school year until this wave. I couldn't throw her in the water and expect her to know how to swim with the sharks. Ms. Scott was already brewing a hurricane in her classroom alone. I was the one who probably would have to call for a lifeguard to get through this. Now I had to figure how to pack all of this into my schedule.

CHAPTER 13

#JUST DO IT!

"I'm home!" I was glad that no one was around. I felt like I could get some real writing done. I still felt the pain from the day's series of unfortunate stutters. Until then, I thought my stutter was improving. It made me so mad that I couldn't speak when I needed to! It's more frustrating that sometimes I was perfectly fluent – meaning without a single trace of a stutter. It's like I wanted to tell my brain to pick a side already! I had so much more to say about it. So much was hidden beneath my stutter that other people can't see. I thought to draw a huge picture of the stuttering iceberg Ms. Plewitt told me about. Also, I thought to describe how I stuttered, what it sounded like, what people saw and heard when I stuttered, and explain exactly how I felt about it. That's the part no one saw. The bottom of an iceberg isn't visible. The embarrassment, the feelings of not being good enough, like no one truly wants to know me after they've heard my stutter, being afraid to stutter, and more. How would I show Ms. Plewitt all of that without creating some boring and depressing memoir of a person who stutters? I was tired of thinking about it! I thought I would feel better to get it out on paper.

It wasn't like Ms. Plewitt put a cap on how much I could write, so I decided to write as little or as much as I wanted. Thinking ahead, if I wrote very little, she'd probably think I was completely okay with stuttering and graduate me from the program before I advance to ninth grade. I already dread losing her to another speech teacher in high school. On the other hand, all of this could also open a new can of worms. "Okay! Enough with the self-talk already. Just do it!" I told myself.

I hoped Ms. Plewitt had her morning cup of coffee and was ready for my story about stuttering. I had diarrhea of the pencil since the first grade, and I was very creative when I wrote. Like Ms. Scott said, "Creativity is Adventure," and writing was mine.

I had an "Aha!" moment, I thought. Adventure was a great place to start. Hopefully, I would discover the good, exciting, and creative side of the adventures in my stutter along the way.

Adventure

Every day is an adventure in my life. The life of Abigail Brewer.

The Merriam Webster Student's Dictionary defines Adventure as:

1. an action that involves unknown dangers and risks

2. an unusual experience

Some of the definitions even include EXCITING but I don't exactly know what that part of it feels like.

Lately it seems like I've only experienced the dangerous, risky, and unusual side of adventure. Lord knows I'm patiently waiting for the day my adventures meet excitement.

Until then, I'll tell you about the other words I've bumped into that describe my adventures.

So, if I could add my choice of words next to the dictionary's definition I would add: dim sparkles, surprising, scary, dramatic, risky, proceed with caution, different, nervous, curious, emotional, bumpy, roller coaster rides, challenging, defeating, broken words, and forever changing.

If I could add a picture and my very own example of the word Adventure used in a sentence as dictionaries always do – I'd glue a huge picture of Abigail Brewer next to it because that's me! All of those words describe me.

The sentence would read: The adventures of Abigail. And STUTTERING would probably be listed as a synonym. That is exactly what stuttering is to me – a not so good adventure!

So, if I had the chance to create my very own entry in a dictionary my personal definition of Adventure would read:

1. a different, fearful, and risky emotional event

Synonym: Stuttering

Plural: Adventures

I'd include the plural form ADVENTURES because I don't just stutter in one particular situation – like when I don't think about how I want to say something, or when I feel nervous, mad, sad, excited, frightened, extra emotional, or glad. Although I do stutter more in those situations, you must understand that I stutter ALL the time! And in more than one way! It has become quite adventurous. It's one adventure after another. In other words, stuttering keeps finding me at times when I least expect it and I am forced to make a decision to be brave, take a risk, and just stutter without worrying about it or let the stuttering win by not saying so much at all. Not saying much at all sounds better to me right now and I'll tell you why.

Today I decided to be brave in Ms. Scott's class. You don't even want to know how bad it turned out. It's like I was stuck in the driver's seat of a car that somebody else was operating. I had no control over how fast or slow my words came out and the passengers had no clue how to help! All they could do was stay in their seatbelts! I wish I could just give them a manual to explain to them what was happening. But, it's never been that easy.

In all of the 14 years of my life stuttering has been the one permanent thing that seems to stick to me like crazy glue. It's there, always has been, and always will be. I guess we're stuck together for life. I've been trying to accept that and see it as a part of who I am, but it is so hard. At times I don't see anything but my stutter! Some days I try not to think about it, but when I begin speaking I am quickly reminded I have to.

Stuttering is tricky for me. By that I mean, sometimes I don't know when or where I'll feel it or catch it in my words. It surprises me. It scares me. It makes me nervous and causes me to proceed with saying other words with caution. This is what dims my sparkle because words are something I know I'm good at. But when you add stuttering and words – you sometimes get a bunch of stuff that doesn't go together – a clash of events! And let's not forget the emotions involved...

You get highs, lows, ups, downs, slopes, and yo-yos. Yes, and no's, stop and go, fast, slow, so-so, and do-si-do. Rainbows, dominoes, hugs, and blows. Tic-tac-toe and no-no, but most of all STUTTERING is what steals the show.

Bright lights, center stage, and front row – stuttering could be my showbiz because I bet I'm well known for it – like a celebrity. Celebrities get special treatment and stand out from everyone else, although the treatment I get isn't the kind you'd expect.

I think I am the only person in my entire school who stutters. That's what makes me stand out. No one ever asks for my autograph or huddles around me like a bunch of groupies with cameras when I walk in the room but I do notice that everyone seems to get awkwardly silent whenever I speak. It feels like the whole world stops.

Maybe it's me, but I think everyone's eyes become filled with questions and they kind of look away for seconds at a time as if they're wondering why I speak the way I do. Oh, and not to mention the infamous SQUINT I've noticed. Yes, some people squint like they can't see and I can't help but wonder how that is going to help them hear me or understand me better? I guess it's their way of thinking with their eyes. It looks so goofy. LOL. It goes against everything I have ever learned about good communication skills in speech therapy. What ever happened to good eye contact?

The wonder in their eyes doesn't look or feel like a good one. It often feels like they look down on me. Sometimes their smiles become phony, like a smirk or an attempt to hold back a bursting laugh. I could be wrong. I just think the worst when it comes to my stuttering. This way I can prepare myself for any whispers, sly remarks, bullying, laughs, or down right evil looks – though I have yet to witness any of that so far in middle school. I guess I just kind of look for that silent bullying in the body language of whoever is listening to me. Their eyes usually tell it all and it makes me feel different when I compare myself – well my speech, to my classmates, friends, family, and the entire universe.

I wasn't always aware I sounded different from everyone else and sometimes I think it was better that way. Maybe I wouldn't feel so weird. Maybe I just wish I didn't stutter at all! Then again, I probably would've never found any kind of adventure – even though I'm still searching for the exciting part of it. So, sit back, fasten your seatbelt, get a travel pillow, and brace yourself to take a rhythmic ride about stuttering with me, Abigail Brewer.

WARNING!

Writing all of this was risky business! If this journal ever accidentally winds up in the hands of someone other than you, Ms. Plewitt, I only want that person to read it if they are courageous and patient enough to really take part in my adventures. It will be a long, and unusual journey, but I think they will find a person they've been wanting to get to know along the way. Maybe they will even find a beautiful, adventuresome, and heroic character they can relate to. And maybe, just maybe find the courage to share their own adventure.

Oh, and Ms. Plewitt, I apologize in advance if I wrote too much or started to make this sound like the start of an epic story. I'm just starting to believe what Ms. Scott said about creativity being my adventure, and this is my way of finding something exciting and creative in this adventure called stuttering.

Mom is making me get ready for dinner...more to come!

♡- Abigail Brewer

CHAPTER 14

#SCHOOL DAYS

The next morning at school, I found the courage to slide my journal under Ms. Plewitt's door before breakfast. It helped that her classroom was next to the cafeteria. I noticed a sign on her door that read: "Do Not Disturb." A clock was under the sign with the time she would be available. I had to wait ten minutes, yikes! She might read it this morning! She's always on top of everything, and from what I could tell everyone in the school loved her! She was always nice and took the time to listen to everyone. She spoke slow and very clear! Maybe that was why I felt so comfortable around her. I never felt rushed or like I must spit out my words when I talked to her. Her eyes didn't squint or wander away from mine when I spoke, too! As I walked away from her door, I felt nervous jitters. My excitement caused goosebumps to form on my skin for the opportunity to finally submit the journal and bring some of this week's drama and my true feelings out in the open!

To my surprise, she passed me in the hallway after I left the morning meeting in my homeroom class. She handed it back to me just before the bell rang for my first period English class. We weren't scheduled for speech therapy again until next Thursday, so I appreciated her reading it immediately so that I can read her feedback about the beginning of my journal. I didn't catch a glimpse of how her face looked as a reaction to her thoughts about my first entry. Her eyes only told me that she was happy to see me and return the journal. What did that mean? I was even more nervous. Did I write too much? I hoped she didn't just stamp a "Fantastic!", "Good Job!", or "Excellent!" on the pages, as some teachers did, on the pages since I wasn't receiving a letter grade. I really hoped and prayed that she didn't expect me to write in the journal like it's a diary. Diaries are so private, and I didn't want to feel like I needed to write about mushy secrets that needed to be locked up.

I anxiously opened my journal to read her response.

Abigail,

Wow! What a great detailed start to your journal. I always love your choice of words and I see your language skills are maturing and blooming like crazy this year. What a creative, interesting, and freeing way to define your experiences with stuttering. I am excited to read so much more. I can feel the rhythm in your rhyme about what feelings stuttering and words create in you. Keep freely expressing this rhythm! I'd like to hear more about your very first adventure. How did adventure get here? How and when did

stuttering become ADVENTURE? Thank you so much for sharing this. It means the world to me!

Sincerely,
Ms. Plewitt

CHAPTER 15

#OH NO SHE DIDN'T!

Hmm? For the first time in my life I questioned Ms. Plewitt's reading skills. Maybe she forgot her coffee, lost her thick-rimmed reading glasses, or read the journal too fast. Did she even read the whole journal entry? She didn't comment on all of it. I poured out my heart about stuttering. She could've at least said she was sorry that I felt this way or agreed that some people look crazy when they look at me while I stutter. If they were in her class, she would grill them about using good communication skills and tell them how important it is to use good eye contact, posture, body language, and little things like looking positive, being attentive, and acting confident. They wouldn't have heard the end of it! Squinting and looking away when someone stutters aren't exactly good communication skills!

I used to look away from others a lot when I stuttered until Ms. Plewitt told me over and over about replacing that habit with effective communication skills. Now, I intentionally tried to look at other people's faces when I talked to them and keep a pleasant looking face, even when I was in the middle of a painful, severe stutter. I noticed that people still stared, squinted, or looked away, but at least I could say I was the better communicator in those situations. Also, I pictured Ms. Plewitt's cat eyes and bright red lipstick all up in my grill while she reminded me about making eye contact whenever I thought about looking elsewhere.

But she's right. It felt good to let out some of my feelings about my stutter for once. A chip was in the ice! She was excited to read more, and now I felt like I could say whatever I felt when I wrote and not worry about how it sounded. She's the only person in the audience, and I trusted her. It took a long time for me to get to that place with her, and suddenly I felt a little positive about that part of the adventure. I figured I'd keep chippin' away at the iceberg and keep the rhythm going. She liked the rhyme poem I snuck in there, too!

After school, I ran to my room to write in my journal again. It's Friday night and I had the whole weekend to write! My mama wasn't going to cut this short tonight! Hmm.... How was I going to tell Ms. Plewitt how "ADVENTURE" arrived here? What did that mean? Did she mean when and how I was born, or how and when I started to see stuttering as a horrible adventure? Either way, it might've helped her to know the story of the very first adventure in my life. It's a juicy one!

Suddenly, I remembered the first assignment in Ms. Scott's class. I fumbled through my book bag, grabbed my notebook, and flipped through my notes. I found it!

This was perfect! This one was a creative and exciting adventure worth writing about. I polished it a little by adding more details, since I didn't have time to finish it in class. Ms. Scott wrote us a letter on the outline of our assignment to tell us what to do. She's my hero for the next journal entry!

The instructions in my notes read:

"Dear Excellent Eighth Graders,

We are beginning the semester with our creative self-expression unit through Poetry. Today I ask that you write a narrative poem. The only rules are to tell a story about your creation. Use onomatopoeia to bring it to life. Make it dramatic, expressive, and vivid! Make it yours. Have Fun!"

CHAPTER 16

#THE BIRTH OF AN ADVENTURE

Rewind! Do you want to know how God wanted me to know He was adventurous and tell the world that, I too, was destined for adventure? Of course, you do! My mom tells the story well, but she also tells it like a mom. It's a big deal. It warms my heart and could make you cry – especially if you knew me very personally. I like to tell it poetically. Ever since Mrs. Scott introduced our poetry unit and said, "Creativity is adventure," I've been able to find adventure in a lot more things in my life – including my creation. I hope it's okay that I'm using some of her work to answer your question about how adventure arrived here. She said we're being graded on how well we let the reader hear our poem without saying a word to them.

Here's my narrative poem of God's idea to birthing an adventure or two.

Click. Beeeeeeeeep.
The dial tone hugs my mother's ear.

Sniff, sif, sif, sniff

Drip, drop, plop sob as tears fill her hands with fear.

Lub, dub, lub, dub

Bu bump, bu bump, bu bump, bu bump, bu bump, bump, bump

Her heart racing.

The doctor said her baby girl won't make it here.

Weep. Whail. Boo hoo.

Gasp. Woooooo. Gasp. Woooooo.

Deep breaths soothe her.

One! Two! Three! Four! Five!

Six months in mommy's tummy is better than none.

But she wouldn't let me move on.

Zzzzzzzzz. Zzzzzzzzz.

Snore. Sleep. Rest. More sleep makes the clock wind.

Six and a half. Seven months.

I think it's time.

Whoosh. Gush. Here I come.

Prayer wasn't a match for anyone.

Push!

Ouch! Ow! Scream! Squall! Screech!

A few more seconds until we meet.

Pop. Slap. Wah Wah.

Awwwwww.

Whew!

Girl. Three pounds. 13 ounces.

Natalie, Nicole, Yolanda, Nope!

Abigail fits such a joyful blessed hope.

Wait. Wait. Five minutes later.

Squirm. Moan. Groan.

I don't think she's alone!

Uh-oh! What? Huh?

You're not done!

Here comes another one!

Push! Push!

Again and again!

Because Abigail now has a twin!

Well ring the bell! That's how I got a twin named Isabelle!"

According to my mama's experience, God must have a great sense of humor and love to surprise people – including her! The entire time she carried us, she said Isabelle hid behind me because the doctors never detected both of us on the many sonograms they viewed during her pregnancy. I overshadowed her entire being. Although mama and the doctors said that was the case, I often wondered if it was the other way around due to Isabelle's personality. Was she the one in the limelight while we were in mama's stomach? I can picture us fighting and shifting positions in the womb just before birth to see who would be seen, held, and heard first in this world. Isabelle must have been putting up a good fight because she was also a breech baby – meaning she came out feet first. One could say that she tried to kick me out the way and accidentally kicked me out of the womb first! Ha! Maybe her personality is based on her thinking that I stole her spotlight, birthright, or something of the sort. I beg to differ. The story of her arrival was scarier, more dramatic, and way more eventful than mine.

Weighing in at only three pounds and quickly dropping down to two, the doctors and nurses immediately grabbed her and had her transported by helicopter to a special unit in a Children's Hospital of St. Louis. This was to keep her alive and breathing because her skin turned purple and blue, and she developed an illness called jaundice. The nurses even had a special way of feeding her because she couldn't suck milk from a bottle. For a while, she had more wires and sensors on her body than actual skin that the nurses had to shave one side of her head to make room for more. Isabelle lived in that unit for another two months before she could share a crib with me at home. I only had to stay in the hospital and cook in an incubator for another month because I had a very hard time gaining weight. It's a miracle we both survived!

Even further before our birth, mama caught a bad infection when she was six and a half months pregnant. The fluid around the sacs in which she carried us became infected. The doctors told her the pregnancy was over. She would not deliver a baby. Still, so much growing and developing had to happen before she delivered; however, the longer she carried, the greater the risks of infection. Then, the doctors sent her to the hospital to treat the infection, but they assured her that the baby had no chance of surviving. Mama said she cried so hard that she probably caused herself to go into labor. Shortly afterwards, she began to leak amniotic fluid from the sac in which she was carrying me. All the doctors kept preparing her for the worst. They had to induce her labor immediately since you can't carry a baby dry. Mama says the only thing for which she prepared her ears was a crying baby. Every time she thought about it, a special peace came over her about the whole situation.

The story is even more interesting. It was near the first week of May when she was admitted in to the hospital. The outside temperatures dropped to a record low of thirty-something degrees. The sky adopted a heavy overcast, and high winds caused the coldest chill in the air. Papa always said that it meant something higher was fighting for us twins. I knew he was right, because it didn't prevent nurses from every floor in the hospital, volunteers, housekeeping staff, friends, and family from making multiple trips there to pray for victory over the odds. Ministers from nearby churches even came to the hospital daily to lay their hands on mama. Nearly a couple of weeks later, at seven months pregnant, she went into full labor.

Being born two months premature caused a lot of medical issues for Isabelle and me for a few years, but I won't get into that right now. Even though the most severe issue of the hello or goodbye for us twins was behind my mama, her new challenge was she now had three baby girls at home who were so close in age that people ask if we're triplets to this day. It is not that we all look alike or anything. YIKES!

My mama had three heads, six eyes, three noses to blow, and three mouths to feed; three cries, six hands, six feet, six shoes to tie; three bellies, three bottoms, and three diapers; and three hearts and three smiles. She had all of this with two hands for three tickles and three giggles! Now that must have been an adventure!

Humor was one of the things that got my mom through it all. My older sister by 17 months, Natalia, didn't think it was funny at all. Natalia always enjoyed having her own space. She liked everything to be where she wanted, how she wanted it, and everyone to do what she wanted when she wants. In her mind, it had to be all about Natalia! The world was hers. She sat on the throne. I believe she thought it would be that way forever until Isabelle and I were born. When we arrived, her world turned into a box of crumbled crayons that she could not put back together. Her days of having her stuffed animals, baby dolls, building blocks, and mama all to herself were over! Queen Natalia knew her reign was over the moment she saw us – *both* of us. Mama said she took a deep breath just before she let out the torrential cry of "Get OUT!" at the top of her lungs. Little did she know that it was a point of no return.

Natalia is still Natalia and loves to keep things perfect and perfectly to herself! Personally, I don't think she ever tried to store the word "share" in her vocabulary. Now that we were getting older, I partially envied her selfishness. Because I was born 5 minutes before Isabelle, everyone called me the middle child! If you know anything about what people say about middle children, it's all true. I had to give, give, give, and share, share, share. I never was allowed to say much about what I wanted or how I wanted things. It's sad, right?

To make matters worse, Isabelle was the baby! We have the same birthday, but my family insisted on calling her the baby. Do you know what that means? She was so spoiled, and she received all the attention that she and I were supposed to be getting together, then Natalia, then me! Suddenly, I felt like I was predestined for an adventure to fight amongst my sisters for the spotlight.

That is how the adventure began. Forgive me if I made it seem like my sisters aren't fun to be around. They really are okay most of the time, and strangely enough they both have some traits I wish I had. Urghhh! I Gotta go. My grandma is calling us for dinner.

♡ Abigail Brewer

CHAPTER 17

#COLLARD GREENS AND CORNBREAD

I ran to the bathroom to wash up before dinner. Isabelle was taking her sweet time playing in the soap while holding the pump bottle to her mouth and singing one of her favorite tunes in the mirror. At that moment I knew for sure she might grow up and try to be an entertainer. She'll need some vocal lessons, but she's pretty good at performing. She always seemed confident, and the family always gave her the attention, smiles, and applauses like she's Beyonce'. I rolled my eyes because I was tired of waiting. As I opened my mouth to ask for the soap bottle, nothing came out. I opened my mouth again... nothing. I was stuck on the hard 'c' sound at the beginning of the word "could." In my mind I knew exactly what I wanted to say; it came out of my mouth very quickly, but unfortunately, that isn't what actually happened. This happened a lot.

I let the beginning sound out, but somewhere between my diaphragm, lungs, chest, neck, the back of my throat, and the sound of my voice, my air and my words were barred from leaving my mouth. Nothing was setting the rest of the word free. I tried three more times. "C-", "C--", "C---." I became frustrated because I was choking on the 'c' sound. I rolled my eyes out of frustration and didn't think Isabelle was paying attention. I didn't notice she had stopped singing. She was looking at me desperately try to get my words out. By then, I was slapping my leg, stomping my foot, blinking my eyes hard, and jerking my head to force the word out. That didn't work! I hadn't used that trick in a long time. I call it a 'trick' because while it worked sometimes, it made me tenser. I stuttered more. Posture, poise, and appropriate body language are just as important as eye contact. I had no reason to move my head, arms, and feet while trying to say the word 'could'. It made matters worse and left me very nervous. I didn't think the word would come out. I'd never get the soap if I never asked, so I must make it come out.

I thought Isabelle knew I wanted the soap, but she continued staring at me with her arms folded. That was a good thing because she was being a good communicator by somewhat waiting patiently for me to get my words out. What Isabelle may or may not have known is that the hard 'c' or 'k' sounds were difficult for me to say without getting stuck. It's probably the one sound on which I could catch myself stuttering the most. I could catch vowels easily, too. To use my good communication skills, I locked eyes with her, took a deep breath, and pushed the words out. "C-c-c-could I-I-I please have the soap?" Because I didn't take a quick but relaxed breath with my belly, I forced the words out. I breathed so hard that my shoulders rose, and my head and neck moved back.

I learned that easy breathing should almost be invisible, unless you stare at someone's belly. Now that I am older, Ms. Plewitt calls it diaphragmatic breathing instead of belly breathing. It's more fun to call it belly breathing because Ms. Plewitt looks pregnant when demonstrates it. I laugh every time.

Ms. Plewitt also would have asked me to modify or change the way I forced the word out and repeat the hard 'c' sound several times. I learned it's called hard stuttering when you force out words and syllable repetitions when you repeat the first sound in words. Additionally, she would have asked me to ease into the word by taking gentle, full-belly breaths. Then hold or stretch the 'c' and 'o' a couple of seconds before adding the other sounds in the word, like "coould." That would have worked for me because it wasn't a trick. Ms. Plewitt says it's a special researched method for getting people who stutter to change their hard stuttering into easier, gentle stuttering. I guess the extra force made it sound like I yelled at Isabelle because when I push words out, my voice becomes louder unintentionally.

Isabelle apparently thought I yelled at her because she responded and yelled, "Okay, you didn't have to yell at me!" "H-h-h-here," she said and slapped her leg! The blank state of shock on my face contained my rage. I found it hard to believe that I took the soap without her running out the bathroom screaming because I purposely squirted soap in her eyes. My mind became flooded with all kinds of thoughts about how to react, but I didn't. I couldn't. Isabelle even stood there for a second as if she were waiting for me to do or say something. I was clothed in disbelief. My twin sister had just mocked my stuttering! My A-one since day one, my ace, my equal, and my womb mate-now-roommate just bullied me to my face because of something she *thought* I intentionally did to her. Tears were desperately trying to fall, but the drops never made it past the whites of my eyes.

I knew it was only going stir the whole family and possibly start a fight between us. All I could say was "I-I-I didn't yell" and watch her roll her neck at me as she walked away. Washing my hands for dinner was painful as I imagined rinsing stuttering down the drain for good.

We all sat down for dinner and inside, I was still crying. My mama noticed my flushed, red face and glossy eyes from trying to hold back the tears.

"Is something wrong Abbie?"

"No ma'am."

In no way was I going to describe what just happened because of my stupid stutter! Mama knew it was something, but to make me feel better she told me my Granny made my favorite meal: bar-b-que baked chicken, collard greens, sweet potatoes, and sweet cornbread on the side. Usually I would be smiling from ear to ear, but this time I immediately thought about turning down my favorite foods. I was afraid of asking Isabelle and my family to pass the collard greens and cornbread because of the hard 'c' sound! The sound made its way from the bathroom to the dinner table. Not to mention we also had cranberry mango juice to drink – another one of my favorites. My heartbeat turned into a stampede of elephants running through the jungle as I listened to my Papa ask Granny to pass him the cornbread. Isabelle asked him to pass it to her next, then Natalia. My turn to ask was quickly approaching. The herd of elephants were running faster and wilder as I wrestled with the idea of jumping in front of them and be trampled in a stutter or dodge them by substituting the words with something else. Fear won because I was afraid to stutter again. With my lips poked out a bit, I had already made up in my mind that I'm going to avoid all of those tricky sounds and ask for chicken and sweet potatoes. Mama must've wanted me to cheer up because she plopped a nice helping of everything on my plate before I could speak. Even though I didn't have to say a word, I felt like I still had so much to say. My journal was waiting for me after dinner.

This evening's entry read as follows:

I wonder about twins. Why do some people get a twin and others don't? How does God make that decision? Before tonight I felt lucky to have a twin sister. Having someone to talk to about all the changes we're both experiencing at the same exact time makes it easier to get through things. I remember when up until about 3 years ago in fifth grade we played Barbie together. It was so much fun having someone else be the voice of the other dolls instead of changing my voice for all of the Barbie dolls if I played alone. We'd make up some pretty funny and creative dialogue. I sort of miss

playing Barbie with her, but let me make this clear... I only miss it because we spent more time together and got along so well most of that time. I don't play with dolls anymore!!! The funny thing I remember is Isabelle and I still would have to change our voices because as twins we sound exactly alike.

We're fraternal twins and don't exactly look alike, but on a good day – if I'm not stuttering too much and you turn your head while both of us take turns speaking – you couldn't tell the difference. I didn't stutter when I played Barbie with Isabelle and I've noticed I don't stutter when I change my voice. Maybe that's what I should've done before dinner. I should've used my favorite English accent to ask for the soap or a Darth Vader voice demanding the soap before I struck her with a lightsaber. We both would've laughed so hard. I was good at making her laugh at times. This time I stuttered so hard when I was just trying to ask Isabelle for the soap to wash my hands. I don't know why or where it came from. Maybe it's because I started stuttering and started feeling tense and nervous because I couldn't get any of words out when I asked her. And it kept happening repeatedly. As you've told me Ms. Plewitt, it might be good for me to try to notice how I am feeling while I speak more often. This time it was hard to stop and do that because I was just so focused on the fact that I couldn't get the words out! So, I used the old tricks we thought we buried last year in speech therapy. You already know they didn't work and resulted in me stuttering even more – like I used to.

As a result, I raised my voice and she thought I yelled at her. You'd be happy to know I did stop to think about how I could have changed or modified the situation by pulling out of the stuttering and then easing back into it, but it was too late. Isabelle made fun of me and mocked me by stuttering and slapping her leg like I did. I was very hurt. I felt like taking the identical Barbies Isabelle and I keep on our desks to remind us of our special bond as twins and destroying them. I wanted to change their clothes and cut the hair on mine. That was very mean of her.

I don't even feel like she would care if I told her she hurt me. And now I think I'm afraid that if I stutter in front of her again, she will mock me again. How could she make fun of something I can't change? Stuttering was God's idea for me not mine! If she had a problem with it, she'd better take it up with my creator! She talked really fast at times and I couldn't understand her, but I politely asked her to repeat herself at a slower rate and she did. Why couldn't she treat me the same way? The sad thing is I knew I'd remain nice to her because that's me. I always covered up her ways. I'm not sure if that's the best thing to do, but no matter how mean someone else is I found it hard to be mean in return. Wouldn't that make me just like them? Maybe I should just resort to being like everyone else. My Papa always tells me to stick up for myself in a nice way. How on Earth do I do that with so many feelings involved? It's easier to walk away and say nothing but if I had to say something to her – the girl who is now just sitting on her bed watching her favorite WWE wrestling show like nothing ever happened, I guess it might sound a little something like this...

Mirror Mirror on the wall

Twin, be nice to me once and for all

I look at you

As you look at me

We're the same can't you see

Any jab, kick, slam, or punch

Thrown my way

Should hurt you just as much

Even though when we fight we don't touch

Your words are a kick in the gut

I could retaliate and kick your butt

But that wouldn't tell you how it really feels and such

I want you to understand

Speaking is something I can't do on demand

It takes a 'k' and sometimes an 'uh' or even an accidental shout

Before I get the message out

The next time this happens I won't pout

I'll tell you how I feel

Without a doubt

Your advice would probably be to talk to my twin about my stuttering. Like one of your daily challenges. It's not fair for me to just let her think I yelled at her when there was a more complicated explanation behind it. If she understood my stuttering and what was happening, it would've saved the day – in a nice way!

♡- Abigail Brewer

CHAPTER 18

#WEEKEND!

Fantastic Family Fridays was a total bust tonight. Part of me was happy we swerved away from the usual of curling up to a good movie on the oversized couch in the family room. At this point, Isabelle had me questioning the definition of family. Mama accepted a promotion at the Post Office that required her to oversee work on the night shift, so she prepared for work a few hours after dinner. I can't say that I liked her absence on Friday nights, but it's better for her and our family because she's saving her money to buy us a new house. I was desperately waiting to have my own room!

Mama and daddy split when I was about three years old, so we moved in with my Granny and Papa until mama could get on her feet. The house was somewhat crowded, and sometimes it felt like we're canned sardines. Moving back to St. Louis from Orange County, California to start over was an adventure in and of itself. I really missed the endless sunny days, the warm weather, and riding my bike in the promenade at our old apartment complex. I was only three, but that feeling is forever ingrained in my memory. I also missed the happiness that came with visiting the beaches as a family.

A couple of years into the move, I remember starting kindergarten at Robinhood feeling like I landed on a different planet. Everything was so new to me. Because of all the changes, I was changing too. Mama told me I took the divorce, the move, and all the changes the hardest of all my sisters because I'm very sensitive – whatever that means. She said I cried a lot at first, and even started to talk less. Then small patches of hair started to fall out of my scalp because of a scalp and hair illness that was said to be caused by stress, called Alopecia Areata. Thankfully, it grew back with medicine and time. Her list went on. Asthma-like symptoms that seemed to rob me of sleep and my voice in the middle of the night were repetitive episodes of Croup, weird vivid dreams, and more. Mama was so worried! Doctors reassured her that it was just stress. It was hard for me to watch my parents be together one minute and completely ripped apart the next. Watching my mama go from being full of energy and bursting with jokes and laughter to being quiet, still, and sad for years thereafter was something I'll never forget. For some reason, I thought I could understand and feel all of what she was feeling just from looking at her. I think the school counselor calls it empathy.

I remember just wanting to do things that made us feel happy because happiness made me forget about all the ongoing changes. I wished that I could ignore the humongous changes that were currently happening.

Is that the reason why Ms. Plewitt wanted to know more about the things happening around me? I was confused. What did that have to do with my stutter? I had to ask her, but not having my mom around wasn't the best feeling. It reminded me of my family being ripped apart again. I wondered if that's why I started to stutter more again? Did rough memories, sad feelings, and too much change cause me to stutter more?

I didn't feel like running with that thought so I wrote it on paper and left it there. I want to end this week on a happy note.

Ms. Plewitt,

Do bad memories, sad feelings, and too much change cause people to stutter more? What does everything around me have to do with me stuttering?

♥ **Abigail**

CHAPTER 19

#ESKIMO KISSES

"Hey twins. I'm getting ready to leave for work. Give me my hugs and kisses," mama said as she walked in our room. Isabelle bounced up out of bed before mama stepped all the way into our room. When she came over to my side of the room, I noticed her badge was upside down. I read it backwards to her to make her laugh because she always looked so serious when she said goodbye to me. Maybe it's because she knew it hurt. "REWERB ECYLA," I chuckled. Looking down at her badge she, couldn't hold back, "Huh, what?" She started cracking up and said, "It's Mom! Not Alyce Brewer to you, Miss Missy." She came closer and gave me a quick Eskimo kiss and tight hug. I instantly felt better about how hard she was working to make all of us happy. She glanced at her watch and ran out leaving us with an, "I love you all" to get us through the night without her.

CHAPTER 20

#READ BETWEEN THE LINES

Instead of going to bed early I thought I'd to try get lost in a good book. Granny never let us go out much, so I probably read, wrote, drew, and daydreamed much more than the average eighth grader. My personal library of books was something to brag about. Over the years I racked up a ton of books because Natalia gave me all her books. They weren't the latest brand-new books, but I didn't care; they're all mine! I appreciate the fact that she had good taste in books and refused to throw them away. I guess she did have the word "share" somewhere in her vocabulary. I grabbed *The Trumpet of the Swan* by E.B. White. It's an old book, almost 50 years old to be exact. I remember Natalia writing a book report on it last year and raving about how good it was. I must see for myself what the rave is all about. Flipping it over, I read the synopsis. Surprisingly, it's about a trumpeter swan who was born without a voice and can't express himself. This was sad because I knew trumpeter swans are known for the beautiful sounds they make. This swan feels so different from all of the other swans that he stays away from his own brother and sisters. He meets another swan and falls in love with her, but he has no way to express how he feels until he meets a boy who helps him communicate by teaching him how to play the trumpet.

Why did I somewhat feel like I could relate to this swan?

I read the book from cover to cover. I woke up with a slightly different view about stuttering.

A lot of students at my school communicate using computers and technology because they must have been born to speak differently, too. Sometimes I used to see Ms. Plewitt working with them. Last year she put on an amazing play with them. Everyone's voice was heard in their smiles, movements, laughter, feelings, and thoughts through technology. I remember thinking none of them appeared to be nervous, afraid, or mad about using technology. They looked like they were extremely happy to be acting in a play and having so much fun. After the show, I told Taylor how cool it was to get to know those students more and see and hear their personalities. Taylor is a neighbor and good friend of one of the girls who was in the play. She's supposed to introduce me to her one of these days.

I started thinking about which is more important: stuttering or using my voice to be heard? For the first time I thought of some positive things about my voice that have nothing to do with stuttering. I can do so much with it. Not with the way it sounds, but what I can say. Ms. Plewitt must've wanted to help me enjoy saying positive things about my voice. She's like the boy in the story who gave the trumpet to the swan. If the swan would've let the sound of his voice get in the way, his love would've been lost. Ms. Plewitt was there to help me and many other students use one of the most important things in life, our voices. I couldn't wait to tell her about the book I read. Come on, Thursday!

Ms. Plewitt,

This weekend I read <u>*The Trumpet of the Swan*</u> by E.B. White. It was such a good book. I was inspired to write a poem to remind myself how lucky we all are to have a voice in this world. I shouldn't be so worried about how my stuttering sounds to everybody else and just enjoy saying what I want to say.

My Silent Voice
Is my silent voice ever really heard
Is my silent voice ever fully heard
Has my silent voice ever heard itself
Or does it just hear everyone else
Does it get lost in the different tones
Or hover around and just watch
Like a shiny little drone
Will my silent voice ever pick up the phone
And get past the dial tone
Has my silent voice ever imagined
Sitting on its own throne
Will my silent voice explore
Difficult things that are hard to ignore

My silent voice wants be part of the move the world needs

You know, like the answer planted in seeds

My silent voice wants to be the one to open the door

For many

And stop along the way

To enter and say

World, let's create a better today

Let's spring up seeds of

Laughter, forgiveness, friendship, trust,

Bravery, memories, ideas, love, and kindness

Using, hearing, and sharing MY voice

With this world

Is a must

CHAPTER 21

#KNOCK, KNOCK, WHO'S THERE?

The smell of Granny's homemade biscuits, bacon, eggs, and grits made sleeping in impossible on this Saturday. Isabelle was at her hip-hop dance class with my aunt, and Natalia was at violin practice. It's eight fifteen in the morning and no one bothered to wake me up to go to my 8 a.m. gymnastics class. That's fine with me because balancing on a beam without the proper rest is a recipe for disaster. I'd wiggle and wobble all over the place. The lack of sleep did the same thing to my speech. I'd skip, jump, bump, and stutter all over the place. It's a good thing no one was around to ask me a million questions. There was a faint snore coming from mama's room, so I knew she was still asleep. "Yep. Out like a light," I whispered while peeking in on her. Papa must have driven Natalia down the street to her private lessons. Granny never had a driver's license and refuses to drive. It was nice to be in a quiet house and enjoy breakfast at the table with Granny while she tried to read her Bible. Usually, she'd be complaining about people calling her and ruining her opportunity to read. Today she seemed to be getting some reading done, so I was careful to not ask for anything.

"Morning Granny," I said while reaching for the Funnies section of the newspaper that laid next to her. Papa probably left them out for me. "Get yourself some breakfast while it's hot!" Granny commanded. Breakfast always reminded me of Saturday mornings in California. Mama would cook enough to feed an army, so all of her friends and their children stopped by for coffee, a bite to eat, and chit-chat. It's usually the same at Granny and Papa's house, but busier and overwhelming at times. I waited to see who's going to walk through the door and pay us a surprise visit. Ten minutes later, a familiar beat knocked on the door. The knock repeated. It's a familiar sound, but I haven't heard that knock in about a year. "Granny, I know e-exactly who that is!" I said with excitement.

As I rose to run to the door, she scolded me. "Sit your butt down! Now you know I don't let you girls ever answer the door unless I tell you to!" My nerves were shaken straight for a minute. I sat at the kitchen table bouncing like a jumping bean in anticipation to see if it was Teddy, my nanny from California. He's such a funny guy. His real name is Theodore, but we call him Teddy because he's so nice and friendly to our entire family. Whenever something is wrong, he makes it his business to do whatever he can to make it better again. Don't teddy bears somehow do that for kids?

When he turned the corner to the kitchen, I sprang up like a chicken into his arms. He smiled and called me the silly name of "Abbie Dabbie

Doo," followed by a big teddy bear hug. It was time for nothing but laughs. He told joke after joke, which made me wonder how some people can quickly make up so many jokes. He noticed I was reading the funnies.

"Tell me a joke, baby girl."

"Okay, okay, I've got one," I said. I knew exactly which joke I'm going to tell him. I just read a good one, but I remembered the one Isabelle told the family a few weeks ago. It still had me going. We were rolling on the floor laughing when she told it. Maybe I was too excited because my chest immediately became tight and I felt a squeezing sensation in my throat like a huge boa constrictor was preparing me for a meal as I attempted to tell the joke.

"A-A-A," I tried to push it out. I couldn't believe I was getting stuck on the first line of the joke. Then again, what did I expect? It starts with my first name – and Abigail begins with a vowel – one of those tricky sounds for me. Teddy maintained eye contact with me as I struggled to get my name out.

"A-a," I said as I tried again. He smiled and told me to slow down. I wished he knew that telling someone who stutters to slow down doesn't help them magically stop stuttering. I proceeded to tell the joke.

This time, I decided to focus on trying to make sure I was starting with an easy, full breath while easing out the 'A.' "Abigail's mother had three k-kids." It worked! Even though I stuttered a bit on that tricky 'k', I didn't want to stop and ruin the joke, so I continued. "The first k-kids name was A-a."

"Amy, Ayden, Ava?" Teddy interrupted.

I can bet my face was blushing like crimson red roses from embarrassment. I hate it when people interrupt me and say what they think I'm trying to say and guess wrong. "No," I shrugged. I had to start from the beginning because a joke isn't funny if you don't tell it with the correct rhythm. I could tell I was losing his attention and interest in the rest of the joke. "Let me start over," I mumbled.

He sat down at the kitchen table. "Sure. But only if you want to. I was only kidding when I asked you to tell me a joke," he comforted.

I knew he wasn't kidding. He's probably trying to give me a way out. Part of me felt like muttering "never mind" and going to my room. Because I liked the joke so much and wanted to be braver with using my voice, I finished telling it.

Easing into it and stretching the beginning vowels a bit longer to make sure I have control over my breath before I finished speaking was working. Replacing the word "kids" with "children" to avoid a bunch of bumps wasn't something I was supposed to do, but it also worked. "Aaabigail's mother had three children. The first child's name was Aapril aand the second child's name was May. What was the third child's name?" This time he didn't interrupt. He smiled and let me get the entire joke out before he said anything. His eyes never left my direction, nor did he look strange. I'm sure he detected the cues of anger and embarrassment I gave him the first time I tried to tell the joke. I felt good, like I could be just as entertaining as Isabelle because my words came out much easier.

"May?" he guessed.

"Nope!" I laughed.

"June, July, August?" Teddy blurted as he guessed again.

Excitement grew in my chest and my voice as I exclaimed, "A-Abigail! It's A-Abigail because it's Abigail's mother who had the three children. Aaapril i-is the first child aand May is the second, which makes A-Abigail the third." I waited for the roll on the floor laugh. It never came. A smile and a few chuckles barely grazed the room. Why was the joke so funny to everyone when Isabelle told it? Was it because I stuttered on the punch line? I wanted to roll on the floor and cry.

CHAPTER 22

#TAKE A MESSAGE: I'M HERE, BUT NOT REALLY HERE!

Time didn't let me hang on to that beat-up punch line for long. Another surprise knock on the door started to rattle me on the inside. This time it was a quick tap then the sound of a key entering the door. It was my Aunt Chrystal, Isabelle, and my closest male cousin, CJ. She must have picked him up from football practice on the way. CJ started telling me about the touchdown he scored at his game. Papa showed up with Natalia and a couple of her friends from violin practice in the middle of his story. Soon after, our neighbor who chain smokes on her porch all the time arrived. I can bet she's here for some black coffee to sip in between puffs. She started asking me about school. The swell of the noisy bodies in the room was making my chest rise. Overly applied musk cologne, mixed perfumes, sweat, a musty uniform, outdoors, cigarettes, and coffee was too much to breathe in at once. Was vomit going to be added to the list after this roller coaster ride? The doorbell ushered in more passengers who stopped to talk to me for some reason. When was this ride going to be over?

Moments after I fastened my seatbelt, the roller coaster car steadied its way up the incline. My sweaty palms, gripped the metal bars while my deep breaths became lost in fear. As the car raced down the hill, my head and hair were sucked into the padded gear, I felt my heartbeat immediately go from zero to one hundred. All of a sudden, the ride came to a halt when the phone rang.

Isabelle startled me. "It's for you Abbie," she yelled. I wanted to tell her to take a message because so much was happening. My stomach was in knots from everyone trying to talk to me and around me, and walking in and out of our house. Talking on the phone was the last thing I wanted to do. Didn't everyone know how much of a challenge answering the phone was for me?

I tried to figure out how to remain calm when the coaster car returned to the boarding station before easing out a gentle, "Hello." I wanted somebody to give me a moment to unfasten my seatbelt! I couldn't find my voice in all of this. I thought, "Should I fight it and jump back on the ride, run from the scene, or freeze and pretend like somebody told me to do the mannequin challenge until the caller hangs up?"

Sweat smears covered the receiver as I grabbed it from Isabelle. My voice, body, and vocal cords felt like they were jammed in a big block of ice. Did anyone have a torch or a blow dryer handy to melt the ice? Hey chain smokin' neighbor! Bring your lighter over here!

I hoped it was Taylor on the other end. I knew no ice would stand a chance of keeping form with her. We'd chat it up about some new song or event that happened at school.

The voice on the other end of the phone said, "Hello" at least three times.

"Ahhhhhhhh," I recognized Taylor's voice and immediately exhaled. Another deep breath of relief followed before I finally eased out a, "Hey Taylor."

"Hey Abigail. Do you think you can come over to my house tonight, or I can come to yours?"

I knew my Granny wouldn't let me go to her house. Granny always said she didn't know how other people run their households. She never wanted to put us girls in situations where we were surrounded by people who don't put kids first. She meant people who yell at kids, rush them to do and say things, or do inappropriate things in front of them, like watching R-rated movies. I seriously doubted Taylor's house was really like that, but you never really know unless you spend a lot of time in someone else's home. When I think of it, Taylor was the only friend Granny allows to spend the night.

"I'll see if you can come over here."

"Granny and Papa said yes."

"Yay! I will have my mom drop me off at 5 or so."

"O-okay. See you later."

"Bye."

CHAPTER 23

#SPIT IT OUT!

Thank the Lord for a BFF like Taylor! She's always right on time. I no longer was fazed by all the thoughts about my joke, a bunch of people talking to me at the same time, stuttering, and the weird feeling of being sweaty and frozen at the same time while stuttering. At least I got through it, and Taylor knew she could come over!

One of best things about Taylor is she's so easy-going, and I don't feel so pressured to be or sound perfect around her. I can really be my nerdy, goofy, abstract, save-the-world self around her. Our time together never seems rushed. She laughs at all my jokes, never interrupts my stories, and shares almost the same creative view of the world.

We make up dance routines, short stories, raps, songs, artwork, and pray for more peace in the world when we go to Sunday School together.

This past summer at camp, we did research poster project and a living museum on movements in India. We studied the history of India, war, The Sacred Tears, Gandhi, Hinduism, Buddhism, Muslims, and so much more. It was so fascinating. Zack, from Ms. Scott's class, gave us neat props to display in the living museum. We wrote about Gandhi and merging his beliefs and practices in the American school system to decrease silent and verbal bullying. We thought that if schools made more people accountable for teaching students to always have compassion for others and always solve problems without violence, surely one day bullying would end. This shouldn't stop at home, with the law, a school counselor and principal, morning classroom meetings, books, churches, or leaders. It needed to start in everyone; everywhere! Didn't we all come into the world kind? Didn't we all somehow learn to be something else?

Taylor and I came to the conclusion that Gandhi would've wanted happiness, compassion, and kindness classes in American public schools because they are the key to teaching us how to think. Somebody once said, "The right thinking leads to a better education."

Taylor and I made up the quote, "Always look for the good in others. Good plus good equals better." It was printed on a poster and framed for the front office at school. We even had a pact to try to be the little changes we wanted to see in our own little world. We often volunteered and helped local business and churches in the community organize events at our school. It was a great way to help promote the importance of coming together. They were always a blast and we got to learn more about different cultures, human welfare, the Bible, and more in a fun way. We often wondered why so much of this was restricted from our classes.

Before I knew it, Taylor was at my door. "Hey Abbie," she said.

"Come on in." My family hugged and greeted her before we ran to my room.

"Where's Izzy?" asked Taylor.

"Probably singing and dancing in the shower like its rain," I responded.

Thank goodness Isabelle wasn't in here, I thought. Izzy would've been attempting to hijack the whole evening! She and Taylor are pretty good friends, too, and I think I'm okay with that. Isabelle befriends all of my friends, and I don't want to have to worry about Taylor and Isabelle becoming BFFs one day. She'd better stay in her lane with this one!

All our laughing sent Granny and Papa to bed early. They should've known we'd be on a sugar high from all the soda, licorice, sugar-coated sour chews, popcorn, and M&M's Papa gave us. Mama hated when he gave us a lot of sugar, but she knew he liked to spoil his girls with sugar, spice and everything nice. He called us Papa's Angels – like the girls from an old movie he had us watch called *Charlie's Angels*. I loved how much he loved us. He's like a father to us. Speaking of M and Ms, I remembered that we had to bring one to church the next day. I was sure I'd remember in the morning or Isabelle would say something about it.

We laughed until beyond midnight as we tried to squeeze in as many games as possible before someone made us go to bed. "Let's get your sisters to play SPIT IT OUT with us," said Taylor. I was surprised Natalia put her cell phone down to join us. Natalia had a leg up on all of us because she was older and incredibly intelligent. Maybe she felt like using her ninth-grade smarts to whoop us in the game. She never bragged about her intelligence, but our family did! All of us took school seriously, so it was anybody's game to win.

Usually when only Taylor and I played the game, we didn't put too much stock into who spit out the answers first. We gave each other a little more time and a couple of extra guesses to answer correctly. We'd guess again and again until somebody figured it out. I guess you could say we cheated to make the game work for us – and that's perfectly okay in our own little, happy world. This was especially true for the algebra questions that made us think.

Taylor read the directions to Natalia and Isabelle, "The oldest player goes first, followed by the player to his/ her left. Roll the color-coded die. The first player reads a question on one of the four academic subject cards color-coded to correspond with the colors on the die. Orange-Math, Red-English, Green-Science, and Blue-Social Studies; the player gets 10 seconds to be the first one to spit out the correct answer. If the player fails to correctly respond the opponents get the chance to spit out the correct answer. The first player to spit out the correct answer gets the points noted next to each question. The player with the most points wins the game. Ready?"

"Let's do this!" said Isabelle.

Natalia picked up the green science card and read, "For 5 points. Any substance that has mass and takes up space is known as?" Of course, she spit out "matter" in the blink of an eye. I was nervous then. I'm used to playing this game with only Taylor and no pressure to spit it out so fast.

Isabelle rolled a blue and read the next Social Studies question, "For 6 points. The name of the Shoshone woman known for helping the Lewis and Clark Expedition in achieving the Louisiana Territory is?"

"10, 9, 8, 7," counted Taylor.

"Sacagawea!" shouted Isabelle. "That question is so third grade," she said as she flipped the card over to make sure her answer was correct.

Taylor rolled the die. "Ughhhh! Not orange," she groaned. Taylor read the next Math question. It was a surprisingly easy addition word problem. She immediately spit the answer out.

I picked up an English card. "Yes, one of my favorite subjects," I whispered! I read, "Words or phrases that mean something different from i-its literal meaning i-is known as?" I knew the answer in a split second, especially since poetry is my thing. My words took too long to come out. Isabelle noticed me trying to force out the short 'i' sound. This time she slapped me on the back and yelled, "Spit It Out" with an evil laugh! I was too late. Because Isabelle popped my back the correct answer came out when the timer rang.

Natalia answered "an idiom" and scored the 10 points. I was furious, but I didn't show it. Taylor knew I was blowing steam. She looked at Isabelle, then looked at me, then at Isabelle again, and then at Natalia, as if she thought one of them would do or say something about what just happened. Nothing was said or done. The game continued for another round before my Papa came in and told us to go to bed. I'd never been happier to obey that order.

That night I pulled out my trundle for Taylor and crawled up to my bed hoping the darkness would hide my tears. I was sure Taylor was upset, too, but once again she knew I just needed space. I should've said something to Isabelle and fought for those points Natalia stole. Natalia was never in the middle of our fights. She usually played peacemaker, so she probably would've handed over the points without a problem. It's Isabelle who would've argued over the points, no matter what. I'm glad Taylor didn't say anything because I expected her to respect Isabelle. After all, it's my fight, not hers.

I didn't know how to fight Isabelle without snatching her and doing the infamous RKO (Randy Knock-Out) wrestling move she's used to watching by St. Louis' own Randy Orton. Judging by the silent river I was crying, I could tell I was getting tired of fighting it. My Barbie doll was waiting for me to chop her hair off! I grabbed it off my desk and snapped the legs out of its sockets! Why does Isabelle treat me like this? Why do I have to stutter so much? I rolled over on my journal.

I clicked on my book light and pressed the pencil so hard to the paper that I almost broke the lead.

Miss Plewitt,

So far, the weekend was a disaster I couldn't clean up. I stuttered with family and friends. I stuttered at times that were supposed to be good. Times like telling a joke, talking to a friend on the phone, and playing a game with my best friend and my sisters. I lost a game because I couldn't say my words in time. Why does the world move against time? Against times like this? For me? The world is quick enough for the quick but too fast for those who need more time. Why does the world move like that? I couldn't keep up. I needed to be taught how to keep up in this unkind war against the world whose victory is speed, or be taken to a place where being still and taking your time is healing, and sisters and brothers are sacred.

I want to go to that sacred place
I want to wipe my tears away to a world where tears are sacred
India
The violent war of two nations necessary for creating peace in many nations
Years in the making
Leading to the world's most tranquil creations
Rivers and water, Sacred and Holy
Can I travel to that place?
Right now?
Water streaming from each of my eyes
To the twin rivers

I want to wash away the salt stains on my cheeks and my heart's cries

In the river that cleanses the pain away and forgives it with compassion and kindness

Lord keep these pure rivers in this polluted world's reach

Keep your promise

To everyone including this girl

With too many cares in my world

I want to go to that place of peace forever

The place where the disrupted flow of words are allowed to flow naturally

Happily

Into the stream and journey to a space filled with light

An ocean with that type of salt

The place where there's no evil sought

The place where the sound of water from my tears

Is powerful enough to drown out the world's war with my words

I want to sail to that school of happiness this August and magnify the bright colors that bring people together

There, only protection, peace, love, and laughter exist with the celebrated bond of my sister

I want to go to that sacred place

CHAPTER 24

CHURCH: #M AND MS

It was too bad I didn't wake up magically sailing away to India to experience their culture of celebrating their brothers and sisters. In India they have a special holiday called Raksha-bandhan to celebrate the sacredness of the sibling relationship. It might've done Isabelle some good to go with me! Until then, I kept believing that one day she would learn to celebrate me in a very sacred and holy place we're going: church! That was the one place that gave me hope to believe all things are possible – even fixing the broken Barbie doll named Isabelle!

We piled into Suzy-Q and parked in front of the church entrance.

"Glad we came a little early to get a good spot," said Papa.

"Yeah, I told you this side of the parking lot would be jam packed if we didn't get here before 9:00 a.m.," said Granny.

"That's right," Papa slapped the steering wheel. "The 6, 7, 8 building is being remodeled, so you gals are stuck with us for a while in church services."

"Will the youth minister or the adult pastor preach today?" asked Isabelle.

"Pastor Daily said he was going to work with the youth minister to finish up the M and Ms series he was working on with you all, then start a new series next Sunday."

"Oh snap! Who remembered the M and M Bible verse we were supposed to have memorized and meditated on? Abigail, did you bring yours? Taylor? Natalia?" asked Isabelle.

"I memorized mine," said Natalia.

"Me too," said Taylor.

"Dang it! I-I forgot to bring it, Isabelle."

"Don't worry, girls. You'll be able to pour out something from your heart once you start worshiping, singing, and praising the Lord. He will supply your every need."

"Okay, Papa," me and Isabelle said at the same time.

I didn't believe Papa was right about that one. I had a funny feeling Pastor Daily was going to do more with our M and Ms than we thought. I felt like he's going to make our M and Ms his Daily Bread during today's sermon! I hear Pastor Daily loves to get the audience involved in all of his sermons—especially kids!

Granny started clapping, singing, and swaying her hips in her purple polyester fitted dress as soon as we made it to the middle aisle. The farther she went down the aisle, the farther her dress rode up her thighs. She was tugging at it the whole time. She and Papa hugged at least fifteen people before claiming seven seats in the second row from the front. They were the most comfortable seats, but I wanted to avoid sitting in the front because I didn't have my M and M verse.

We all slid past an elderly couple one by one. Isabelle sat between Taylor and me. I turned around and noticed Mama talking to a lady whose face I couldn't see through the crowd. She must have talked through two songs before she came and sat with us.

"That was Ms. Plewitt," she said as she shuffled around and situated herself next to me."

"Really?" I responded.

"Yes. She said she's visiting churches in the area in hopes of finding a new church home. I told her you were up here, but she said she didn't want to have anybody move out of any seats for her. She's going to come to talk to you after the service."

I was cheesing from ear to ear. Even though we just started coming to church regularly, I knew she'd love it here just as much as I did. I thought to go sit in the back with her so I wouldn't be put on blast about my M and M verse! The congregation was so big that I was sure to be in the clear back there.

The once lit room dimmed. Colorful stage lights came alive. Drumsticks struck the cymbals with four swishy and glassy clangs. "One, two, three, four. Are we ready for some worship?" the lead worship singer screamed in the microphone.

The congregation went crazy. Spotlights flickered as the choir belted out a harmonic, "Whoa, oh, oh, oh, oh." The crowd repeated. The projector screens displayed the words to the song and glimpses of everyone singing and stretching their arms to the ceiling.

Every kid, tween, teen, and young adult jumped to their feet and started rockin' out at the beginning of the song. The elders and Granny and Papa looked confused. "They're about to sing one of the songs we usually sang in 6,7,8. We sing it a lot in the car," I told mama. The blazing electric guitar, electric keyboard, and rippled beats on the drums turned the room into a live gospel rock concert. Taylor and I couldn't hold back from pumping our fists and jumping up and down to the music. You know Isabelle was trying to show off her vocal skills. Natalia actually has the prettiest voice in the family, but she wasn't feeling well. She was boppin' her head to the music from her seat.

"This is for all of the 6, 7, and 8's in the room!" the lead worshiper announced.

"We had to make it up to you for taking your space from you for the next few months, but praise Jesus for the new ground breaking of an epic state-of-the- art youth center with a special space just for you kids in the middle! The Bible tells us that patience is one of the nine fruits of the spirit, so if you're patient with us for a few weeks you're going to be screaming for joy when you see the good fruits that are being prepared for you in that center," he continued.

Taylor nudged me and said, "That's what my M and M was about!"

We all cheered in response to the worship leader's message.

"So, without further ado, let's worship His holy name. Put your hands together, raise them high, sing, somebody scream!

Everyone clapped and slapped their hands to the beat.

We all sang with the words on the screen.

By the time the song was over, Granny and Papa broke out into a full-blown sweat from dancing so hard. The ushers started handing out paper fans to get us through the next four worship songs. I noticed Pastor Daily and First Lady's faces were plastered on the front and back of them.

After the opening prayer, Pastor announced for all of us to turn around and greet each other. Everyone was still worked up.

Several eyes were closed. Heads and hands were lifted high. Prayers were spoken in foreign tongues. Big, colorful hats bowed low in the pews.

Sisters kneeled in the aisles while their praises bounced off the metal rafters. The sunlight shone through a big transparent image of a dove on the bright and color-stained tempered glass windows, and the choir's echoes filled the room. After we sat down, people were hugging and crying. It was like a strong wind blew love all over the room.

I heard some parents fussing at their kids for goofing around. Granny snatched Natalia's cell phone from her. "Pay attention!" she scolded.

"Who's hungry for some Daily bread?" Pastor Daily shouted with a huge grin on his face.

"Well, I'm not gonna start off with your entrée today. I'm not feeding you dinner without yo appetizer. In fact, today you are getting dessert first! Somebody give me an 'Amen!' if you want your cake before yo bread and yo cookies before your sandwich because I do!"

"Mmm mmm mmm," he sang along with the pianist striking chords on the electric organ.

"It's about to get like Campbell Noodle Soup up in here! 'Mmm, mmm good," Pastor said as he rubbed his belly.

"The tweens and teens are about to serve y'all today!"

"You see, you parents and older folks might think some of these tweens and teens aren't so shiny on the outside right now and filled with who knows what, but they're about to show you just how good and sweet they are on the inside!"

The grown-ups chuckled.

"Who's ready for some M and Ms? I know I am! It's gonna be my favorite day today because you see, this big ole family size bag of M&M's? They're all mine and I ain't sharin'. I get to eat all of em' during this whole sermon," Pastor said as he shook up the bag. He poured a few in his hand and tossed them around like he was about to roll lucky number sevens on a pair of dice before he popped a few in his mouth.

"Mmm mmm mmm," he said smacking, "God knew exactly what He was doing when he created these lil' scrumptious thangs. They're perfect! Crunchy and colorful shells on the outside that can hold up in the heat, and a delightful chocolate filling on the inside that melts in your mouth. I hope you brought your own M and Ms today!"

He paused, rubbed his hands together, and looked at us like we were tasty little morsels. I was more scared. Taylor told me to just use her verse if he called on me.

"You see, all of these red, blue, green, yellow, orange, and brown M&M's represent all of us in this world. But I'm here to tell you today – the shell ain't the best part! In fact, if you never knew anything about M&M's, you might be fooled to think it is. You would have no idea that the best part is in the middle. The only way you get to know the inside is the best part is by studying it, reading the label, reading the descriptions, then taking a bite for yourself. After you take a bite you get to taste the goodness. That goodness just makes ya smile and feel good."

"The middle is the core. It's your heart. Can people expect to find the same goodness in your heart that's inside M&M's? Sure, they can! I bet they can find something even better! Tweens, teens, you ready to pour out all of that goodness inside you?"

"Okay teens. No getting shy and trying to hide in your shell today! We about to turn up the heat, and I want you to know you can withstand it! We're gonna actually get rid of your shell today to get to the good stuff. Push three of your neighbors and tell em', 'I'm coming out of my shell.'"

"I'm coming out of my shell," I turned and said to Isabelle and my mom while giving them a gentle push. Isabelle pushed me a little hard, but I just ignored it.

"That's right! You all have this nice and shiny outer shell that you might think defines you. You might think it's the best thing about you. Maybe you think it's all other people see and care about – even down to the color that melts right off as soon as you put in in your mouth. And did you know that the color and dye on M&M's is tasteless? About as tasteless as bland old oatmeal! Once that color is gone, you're left with the same shell as everyone else. Again, I'm here to tell all of y'all the best thing about you is inside."

"Is everybody okay with showing us what's inside of your shell today? I just know it's as sweet as the insides of these milk chocolate M&M's! I mixed in some caramel, almond, peanut butter, crispy, and peanut M&M's too. I hope it won't cause an allergic reaction to others, cause' some of y'all can get a little nutty from the nut that lives inside your shell! Yes, I know some of these tweens, teens, and folks in our house is just plain ole' nutty. But that's okay – yo Pastor can be a little nutty and crazy too at times!"

A nut was definitely housed in Isabelle's shell, I thought.

Pastor Daily couldn't hold back from laughing. He spit out a couple of M&M's on the stage from laughing so hard.

"Here's how we are going to do this. 6, 7, 8's if you wrote down your verse you were instructed to memorize and Meditate on, take them out and read them to three neighbors around you. If you have it memorized that's okay too."

"Whew! I'm out of dodge!"

Taylor turned to Isabelle and I and said, "The fruit of the spirit is love, joy, peace, longsuffering, kindness, goodness, faithfulness, gentleness, and self-control." (Galatians 5:22, ESV).

Pastor was looking my way, so I turned to my mama and abbreviated what Taylor said to me.

Isabelle repeated what Taylor said. The First Lady flashed a wide smile, hugged us all, and turned back around in her seat.

"First Lady, why don't you bring your sweet self on up here," Pastor Daily flirted.

"Don't she look good y'all? Like one of those good ole' homemade peach cobblers fresh out of the oven? Right?"

"I picked out this sweet candy of a wife all by myself, but you middle school boys better not be thinking about picking out any girl candy right now. Yo candy better be yo Bible, yo books and basketball! Shoot, that's another sermon for another Sundee I'm not gonna go into right now!"

"For now, come on up here bae'."

I could tell he was embarrassing her by her blushing pink cheeks, but she looked like she's used to his silly southern twang. They're both from the South. They relocated to St. Louis a few years ago.

First Lady walked to the pulpit in her pointy-toe heels and white, fitted wide-legged slacks. She's so pretty, I thought, and her outfit is on point. Pastor turned to her and asked, "Did you have any leftover M and Ms from these tweens and teens you mind sharing with me and the congregation? I know I have my own bag, but the pew needs to get their fill too. Don't be stingy," he laughed.

She accepted the mic and began speaking.

"I do, I do, I do. I just want to say how great it was to watch you kids enjoy turning and talking to one another with confidence in the Lord's scriptures. Nobody shied away or laughed their way out of it. Thank you for giving me a glimpse inside your shell. I want you to know that you can always have confidence in God and lean on His sweet words inside the Bible to support you in times of need. The M and Ms I heard were amazing. I felt the Holy Spirit's guidance in each and every one of you as you read or recited your verses to me. Those verses stood out to you for a bigger reason, and God wants you to hear everything He is telling you about the scriptures you picked out. You just have to keep opening your heart, eyes, and ears and LISTEN! Listen to the messages inside your Bible."

She continued, "I heard a couple of Bible verses from these beautiful young ladies in the front row. When I was growing up, I remember having those same scriptures stuck to my bedroom mirror on sticky notes. I think I called them sticky prayers. My mama made sure the word stuck to me for more reasons than one. I had to learn to hear the Word, do the Word, and pray the Word. Believe it or not, it took my Mama and Papa to crack a few whips over my shell to get to this sweet place God wanted me to be. It was painful at times, but I am so thankful to this day to know that every shell God has to crack to get to a better place in life He always puts completely back together. It becomes something new and filled with the best fruit. Then it produces more good fruit for everyone else."

Pastor chimed in. "Parents, you know exactly what days she's talkin' about. The days when yo teen is actin' up and you send their behinds straight outside to pick out a switch from a bush to beat the shell right off their bottom! Some of ya'll are young parents, so you try to use those weak things called time out and punishments! We need to go back to the old days!" He came and stood directly in front of me, Isabelle and Taylor. He looked directly our way. I thought, "Yes! He is talking all

117

about Isabelle! Isabelle better listen up before she gets a whip cracked over her because she could definitely use some kind and gentle fruit inside her shell!"

Pastor walked off the stage with another mic towards us.

"Man, oh man, boy oh boy, oh boy, oh boy, oh boy. It's going down! Lord have mercy on me! Please don't come askin' me to say anything," I whispered to myself.

"Whew!" First Lady continued talking.

"The first one was all about the fruit of the spirit which is love, joy, peace, patience, kindness, goodness, faithfulness, gentleness, and self-control."

She continued, "That is a powerful verse beyond measure. It's saying there is a sweetness in showing your fruit of the spirit! I know none of us are perfect and we might not always show others our best fruits—especially during our tween and teen years. Sometimes it's a part of growing up. But that's when God continues to show His loving mercy and kindness and His Spirit guides us to our sweet spots. The Spirit lets us know when we're on the right track by the goodness it brings to our life and the lives of those around us. Simply put, good fruit on the inside produces good fruit on the outside. God wants to fill you with his best fruit no matter how hard your shell is at the moment! The thing is He wants others to see that sweetness that's on the inside too."

Pastor Daily jumped in again, "You see this Bible? It looks just like an ordinary hardback book on the outside, but when you gently open it you discover it's filled with something sweet. When you read it, try to understand it, memorize its scriptures, meditate on its ways and practice what's written – you taste the sweet, tender, loving and kind gifts the Lord put into it. That same love and kindness created you, and LIVES INSIDE YOU! Can I get an Amen?" he shouted.

He backed up a bit and looked around the room.

"Listen! I want you to leave here today and never look at M&M's the same way. Look at them as reminders to Memorize and Meditate on the sweet words in the Bible because it's gonna help you big time in this world that can be everything opposite of the nine fruits of the Spirit. There is a battle going on between the world and your good fruits daily and you cannot let the enemy in that precious shell of yours. The enemy wants to attack everything good in you! Don't you wanna win? Well let me assure you this is one way to win. Let love and kindness conquer. So when the haters hate show em' 'what's good' as y'all teens would say in slang. Show em' kindness is good. Joy is good. Love is good. Humility is good. Honesty is good. Faith is good. Self-control in situations where you have to make the right decision in difficult situations is good and more. All I'm sayin' is that these are good things to have because they are exactly what Jesus has. Who in the buildin' wants to be more like Jesus?" he paused and eyed the whole congregation.

I did not expect Pastor to do the nutty thing he did next. He startled all of us and dumped about a fourth of the bag of M&M's candies on the stage! Then he asked a couple of kids to come up on stage, telling them, "Step on em.' Stomp on all of these M&M's. Smash them to pieces!"

"He continued, "You see this mess? This is what happens when you let the enemy inside your shell! This is what you teens call 'a hot mess.' There is nothing cool about these candies anymore. They're all jacked up and cracked up and need a miracle to be cleaned up and put back together. The good news is the Lord is a miracle worker and is waiting to remold em', refill em', and restore em' to something new. Stand up and shout, 'restoration is real!' You're never too jacked up and cracked up for Jesus to fix and use for something great!"

I could see spit flying out of Pastor's mouth. This was getting good, and Isabelle was probably burning up on the inside!

"Pastor is on fire today," said a lady behind me.

Pastor sent the volunteers back to their seats, calmed his voice to a string of harmonic piano keys, and stood over to us.

"You see, we all have something so sweet on the inside the world needs, but who will be bold enough to let their shells completely go and let their light shine for Jesus through and to this dark world?

He raised his voice again. "Let me put it to you even more simple because I feel like somebody really needs to hear this today.

I looked at Isabelle.

Sons and daughters, we all have to leave those dark dim ways at the door because fighting, killing, bullying, disrespectin' yo mama, daddy, teachers, friends, and family members, stealin', worshipping video games, cell phone apps, celebrities, cars, clothes, and shoes are dimming the light and hardening the shell of many! Bust out of yo shell! You ain't never too young to bust out of yo shell! Amen!"

The organ sang. The congregation roared with banging claps and stomps. "Preach, Pastor. Preach," yelled a man in the front row.

Pastor came back and stood in front of us.

"Are you all sisters?"

Taylor pointed her right and left fingers at Isabelle and I. "They are twins."

"Twins? Oooooh I feel like preaching today! Identical or Fraternal?"

We looked nothing alike, so I thought it would be obvious to him.

"Fraternal," Isabelle responded in the mic.

"How do you two like being twins?"

He held the mic to me.

"It-It's okay."

"You may not understand this now, but the power of two or more coming together is so powerful and significant. I know the two of you probably fuss and fight like most siblings now, but I encourage you to get to the sweetness of the power of two in your lives. Show nothing but love and kindness toward one another as you get older."

He started to whisper a bit and told us, "I'm gonna tell you two that both of you are blessed to be here! One of you needs the other more than you think right now. Both of you have a magnificent light to shine. One day you will touch many lives. The world will see and hear one of you in the most unexpected, gentle, but loud ways. You both will look past your shells and come together to make this happen. That light will never be dimmed."

Isabelle and I looked at each other as the congregation filled the room with, "yes, Lord", "we agree, Lord", "touch these young girls, Lord", "I declare it, Lord."

Pastor left us with a mighty, "In Jesus' Holy name! You haven't seen or heard what the Lord has in store for you! All of you, everybody – bust out of your shells today! Let's all come together in prayer and finish being fed the daily bread. Who's ready for the main course? Who's ready for good ole' Southern fried chicken?" Come on y'all. Y'all know I love some fried chicken! Sweetie Pie's, here I come! Just hold on til' after this sermon!"

After the benediction, Pastor told us to be sure to get a travel sized pack of M&M's with the nine fruits of the spirit taped to them for us to memorize and meditate on this week on our way out, and he announced he would be preaching on the story of David and Goliath next week.

Our homework was to think about the goliaths or giants in our lives right now. He explained that Goliaths are big challenges we're afraid to face.

CHAPTER 25

#A HARD NUT TO CRACK

As we got in the car, I thought about what Pastor Daily said. What did he mean? How did he know Isabelle and I were fighting, and she was dimming my sparkle? How did he know that we almost died at birth and were blessed to be here? Maybe he talked to Papa beforehand. Who is going to be seen and heard by the world? How on Earth would Isabelle and I come together? I felt bad about ripping apart the Barbie; I thought I should put her legs back together.

I waved goodbye to Ms. Plewitt. She was smothered in the crowd too, making it hard to find her after church. The whole ride home Isabelle kept talking about how she always knew she'd be a star one day. She even had the nerve to say I will be her fashion designer or something and touch many while she touches millions! Ughhhh! "There were so many reasons why I couldn't get past her shell! Do I need to stomp on her to get to her good side?" I thought as I rolled my eyes at her behind her back. Maybe I needed a nutcracker!

CHAPTER 26

#DEATH BY LESSON PLANS: JESUS TAKE THE WHEEL!

I couldn't believe it was already Wednesday and I had nothing planned for the speech therapy session with Abigail the next day. Normally, I was the Type A, plan-it-all-to-the-T person who had it all together! I felt more like the Type F, free-flying type of person since I read Abigail's first journal entries. She really surprised me this past Monday morning when she turned in the detailed entries she made over the weekend. Her poetry is moving for her age. It seems like her poetry is becoming as deep as her feelings. It is rhythmic to her experiences, and it seems to flow so naturally for her.

The problem was I had no idea how she felt about stuttering. We talked, laughed, and joked so much during our weekly one-on-one sessions. She seemed so happy. Talk about the part of the iceberg you can't see under the water that I completely ignored. There, underneath the tip of

Abigail's iceberg, so much more was happening. She's facing fear, embarrassment, a borderline bully of a twin, a fast-paced and fast-talking household, anxiety, and she's comparing herself to those around her! She's also worried about what her peers and family members thought about her stuttering. I was ready to graduate her from my program! She now needed me more than ever. I felt like I failed one of my favorite students. Lord, forgive me. Help me. She was the first teen student with whom I worked who stutters, and things have changed so much. When she was younger, I used to pick her up on the weekends for play dates with my daughter. We'd play games and go to restaurants. It instantly became a therapy session, and I had the chance to encourage her to be more confident in other environments. This stopped when one of the teachers saw us and snitched. Mr. Bee thought it was a conflict of interest and liability if something happened. Some people know how to ruin a good thing!

I felt like I needed to start from square one, but I didn't know where. I panicked. None of this was in my text and reference books. Was this the point in my career about which my college professors warned me? The point when I will wear more hats than the SLP one? I was a counselor, a friend, a coach, a cheerleader, a motivational speaker, a comedian, a singer, a play partner, an artist, a writer, a human dictionary, a computer programmer, a spy, an explorer, paparazzi, an actress, and a clown who made silly faces. Whatever the name, I was supposed to wear it. Was I supposed to be a chameleon, a transformer, or the shapeshifting mutant lady from the X-Men? The good news was I was willing to wear any hat

I needed to help my students become good communicators, but I couldn't figure out which hat was the most appropriate for Abigail.

I needed to call for a lifeline! I needed a stuttering specialist on speed dial! Where in the world was my fluency professor from graduate school? Where was that famous lady on all my best fluency materials? Where was that amazing SLP dude from all the online videos? Where was the link with all the answers on the websites for people who stutter? I wondered if it was weird to google their contact information and send them an email message? I couldn't do that! I'd surely be the one person who was fired for sharing student information. I didn't know what to do next. We were a few weeks away from her IEP meeting and the Performing Arts Show! I was running out of time. I needed to breathe! I told myself to snap out of it.

It's time to go deep and let my feet touch the ocean floor. I couldn't continue swimming with the same ole' fish. Abigail wasn't swimming with tiny goldfish anymore! She's in a new school and I had to swim with her.

I was right about her beginning to notice things she probably never knew existed in her world of stuttering. She was very aware of everything going on around her, how stuttering made her feel, and how she stuttered! This was good, but I knew she would notice if I came into the classroom unprepared and try to wing it the next day. I also knew she noticed I wasn't sure how to respond to her journal entries, too. I must have done something right because I did get her to keep writing. I thought I was having a panic attack! I breathed in and breathed out over, and over again. I was starving for oxygen. I couldn't think. I prayed to God that Jesus lead the way, take the wheel, and help me pick this apart and solve the problem.

I took out the copies of her journal entries. The ink smudges from me blacking out names and her personal information ran down the page, making it a little hard for me to reread it.

"How am I going to help Abigail calm the waves crashing and splashing over her right now?" I thought.

I thought I identified that she just wanted to be okay with her stutter, and find creativity and some good adventures with it. The journal was my evidence! I needed a plan to make sure she found this creativity and adventure, but I didn't think I had a creative, poetic bone in body! I needed more information. I needed more observations. I was starting to sound like a scientist on a quest to speak Abigail's language of stuttering! I had Mr. Bee to thank for that!

I thought about the conversation I had with Mrs. Schivers, my prayer warrior. The Lord told me to believe and listen.

That's it! I thought it might be good for me to just listen and observe. Had I ever just listened to Abigail? Looking back, I probably ran my mouth for 20 of the 30 minutes in some of our sessions. That was not good! That's what these waves were all about anyway: listening, observing, and learning! I couldn't talk and truly listen to someone at the same time and expect to fully understand what they are telling me. If only I would've been listening to Abigail more closely all this time!

I decided to give it all to the Lord. I followed His footsteps. I was going with the flow of Abigail's waves! As my professor used to say, "Go with the flow. Don't do what everyone else does. Your student isn't everyone else!"

CHAPTER 27

#THE INTERRUPTION OF EVERYTHING

"Come on in Abigail." I said as I glanced up at the clock next to my huge poster of an iceberg. It made me immediately think about shattering the block of ice!

"You're right on time. How has your day been today?"

"It's been okay."

"Do you want to talk about anything?" I said as I tried my best to hide the fact that I had no clue where this session was going.

"A-a-a-a-c-c-c A-a-c-c-t-t A-aaactuully I-I do."

My heart dropped. I hadn't heard Abigail stutter so hard in a couple of years. "Jesus where were you?" I thought.

"Sure. What is it?" I responded.

"What did you think of my last j-journal en-en-tries?"

I didn't know what to say. I had to think quickly.

"Abigail, I am so thrilled that you are opening up to me about your life and your stuttering. I am even more excited and interested in what you think about your journal entries. It seems like you are learning a lot about yourself, too, by writing in the journal."

I didn't know what I was saying. I asked Abigail a question and she answered my question with a question.

I noticed the awkward silence between us for a couple of minutes, so I started speaking again. "Being able to express your feelings, fears, and ups and downs in such a creative and positive way takes courage. There are a lot of people in this world who could learn something from you." I said to Abigail. I didn't know where those words came from – I continued.

"Tell me, how do you feel when you write?"

I hoped Abigail didn't think that I had asked her a trick question. She probably thought the answer should've been a no brainer to me.

"Umm, Umm, uhh, I think I feel aaalll k-k-kinds of different ways. First, it's like I get to be me, and I'm not scared to let the paper really get to know me. When I stutter, people don't always really get to know me because they are sometimes in a rush to talk over me, speak for me, finish my sentences, or, or just take over the whole c-conversation. Or some people just seem so unc-c-comfortable with my stuttering that they don't talk to me that much a-at all. B-but mostly I-I feel a little sad because I just want the people around me to slow down. I-I want them to understand stuttering. I want them to be okay with it. I-I guess I want stuttering to be a normal thing in this world."

"How do you feel when you're finished writing?" I asked.

I could tell Abigail was starting to notice that we weren't doing our normal routine of talking about funny stuff, and practicing phrasing, pausing, and smoothing out her speech. I purposely wanted to ask her more thought-provoking questions.

"I-I guess I feel better. I mean, I feel like I k-kinda let go of some of the bad feelings about stuttering when I'm done writing. I-I feel like I've won the war going on with my words because my words come out so smooth and creative on paper."

"If you could have one goal to focus on this year, what would it be?"

Abigail looked up at the iceberg poster that was the focus of about three speech sessions the year before.

"I-I guess it would be feeling better about my stuttering and getting other people to be okay with stuttering."

"Well. I think those are some excellent goals. I'm committed to helping you reach these goals in any way possible this year."

"O-okay."

"Now. I want to help you map out how to get there. It will be sort of like our own adventure. We will need tools, a legend or key telling us what to do when we get to certain points in our journey, and rewards along the way for getting past certain obstacles. We might even need certain people to join us along the way."

Abigail smiled so wide when I told her this. Wow, I thought. I just initiated a plan for Abigail to find adventure in her stuttering. I knew that was the Lord's helping hand. I immediately thanked Jesus!

"Let's get to it. Let's start where we're at. Let's get creative. Let's get dangerous. Let's be brave, defeat some giants, and taste victory!" I said to Abigail. She laughed and looked at me with a sense of hope in her eyes. "We can do this! We will do this!"

"Ms. Plewitt, how are we going to do this in 30 minutes a week?"

"Don't worry Abigail! Trust me, I will find you and show up in the places you need me be!"

For the remainder of the session, we wrote our goals, and I wrote some things for Abigail to tackle along the way.

CHAPTER 28

FEAR

I ran to Ms. Scott's class and plopped in my seat seconds before the bell rang. Sweat beads were all over my forehead, and I felt like I needed a shower. I hate feeling rushed. It always seemed to set off the sprinkler hose in my body, which is horrible on cheer uniform days! I caught TJ looking over at me as I secretly tried to take a whiff of my armpits. He laughed to himself. I smiled back, but I wasn't amused at all. His cute dimples had me blushing; they give me a giddy feeling all the time. I wished I could get to know TJ better. He seemed so chill and cool all the time like nothing bothered him.

"Class, class," Ms. Scott said as she grabbed our attention.

I immediately snapped out of my daydream that was probably about to go off the rails.

"Yes, yes," we all responded.

"Are you ready?"

"We're ready (clap), to do (clap, clap), what we came here to do (clap, clap, clap)."

"Great. Well then, let's get started."

Ms. Scott walked closer to us and sat on her pink, plush-decorated wooden barstool. She put on her fuchsia-framed reading glasses and began to read a few famous poems about fear. She read Maya Angelou's *Still I Rise* and let us watch a video of a teacher reciting a poem. She then let us watch a 12-year-old recite what had to be the best poem of all time before reading one of her very own pieces.

Fear
From me to you
To me from you
This is what this invisible thing called fear thinks it has the power to do
It swoops up and down to and from the skies
To tell you tons of little lies
Are you surprised
It then shapeshifts and takes on your form of disguise
It colors your hair, it blushes your cheeks, and glosses your eyes
It plays basketball with your heart and shoots at it to deflate it like a dart
Are you surprised
It turns up the heat and leaves you with stinky sweaty armpits and feet
That's what it calls a smell of defeat
Are you surprised

It wants to hug you to get close enough for you to hear those little lies

For it knows you are more wise

It looks down on you, your hopes, your dreams, and your talents

Its goal is to traumatize

Are you surprised

Let me be the one to emphasize

No matter how hard it tries

To leave you in chastise and horrifies, unable to vocalize

And hypnotize you with its lies

Young person, I want you to realize

You have the power

To keep it from taking over

Are you surprised

I'm not, because I tell you fear has made its way to all of us at one time

or another

But the beauty of it is

It mystifies but never justifies

How high

You will rise

The whole class stood up, snapped their fingers, and clapped. I thought Ms. Scott was my ultimate hero. I wanted to be just like her and read my poetry to everyone one day. It was jam-packed with so much rhythm, rhyme, and truth. She was telling her truth, and I felt every line of it. I wonder what she feared when she wrote it.

"Ow, Ms. Scott has that fire!" TJ yelled.

Ms. Scott's eyes watered from joy because we all loved the poem so much.

Her voice was shaky as she reeled us all back in to pay attention to her next set of instructions. She rolled the smartboard out of the way so we could read, "Today we are going to take a ride with fear" on the board.

Ms. Plewitt unexpectedly walked in the classroom and sat at the back of the room as we started to read.

She didn't sit next to me, so I didn't think she was there to pull me out of class. I didn't think I would have agreed to leave this class if the building was on fire. She would have to use the Jaws of Life to free me out of my seat. Ms. Scott had me hooked on her lesson.

Ms. Scott looked at the board and asked us to read what it said in unison.

"Creativity is your Adventure. Creativity is fear waiting to be set free. Is fear holding you back from discovering those hidden treasures and letting the world see them shine? Do you have the courage to set it free?"

No one looked confused about this one. It clicked for me right away.

Was I letting my fear of stuttering rob me of all the great things hidden inside me? Was I allowing my stutter to dim my sparkle that much? Was I allowing my stutter to stop me from being more creative? Was I allowing fear to remove me from my own exciting adventure? A light bulb turned on in my head.

Ms. Scott carried on, "Who knows what tools we need to keep fear tucked neatly in its place?"

Taylor raised her hand and said, "We can't just slay it for good?"

"Well that's a good question," replied Ms. Scott.

"Since fear has made its way to all of us at one time or another it's important to remember that at times it's there for good reasons. It keeps you out of trouble, keeps you from doing or saying the wrong things, and could save your life if a bear was three feet away from you. Fear can also help push you beyond your personal limits once you become aware of it. It can help you grow, achieve, overcome, and get you out of your shell – as long as you let the tools of courage, bravery, and power take the ride with you."

We all looked confused again.

"What I mean is you must be okay with feeling fear at times and just do the things you have your heart set on doing anyway. You must realize you have so much power over fear. You have a choice to let it stop you from finding adventure, and being your most creative self, or to face it. Do not fear, fear itself! It may be the lion, but it's in a cage! Let it roar. It can only hurt you if you let it. It isn't the ringmaster or the conductor. You are! Your creativity is!"

"Any questions?" Ms. Scott asked as she flashed her bright white veneers at Ms. Plewitt.

"Great! Let's get in your focus groups. Once you are in your groups, I want you all to write one poem addressed to fear that includes all your voices. You may either write one that all of you contributed ideas to or use a tag-team or round-robin approach in which one person says the first line, the next person does the second line, next person third line, and keep going around until your poem is finished. There should be no individual poems. Tell your truths and let your voices be heard! Ms. Plewitt will be coming around to each group to help."

CHAPTER 29

#TAG! YOU'RE IT!

"I'm about to spit some bars. I just need some beats," said TJ as he started tapping the desk and beat boppin'.

"We have to do this together and we weren't instructed to write a rap song. I like the idea, but we just have to do what she said," interjected Zack.

"I'm sure your rhyming skills will come in handy TJ!" said Lauryn.

"For sure!" said Imani.

"So where do we start? What are you all afraid of?" asked Zack.

"Abigail, will you record everything?"

"Sure!"

"Now let's see, what is everyone afraid of? Let's start there," said Zack.

Imani blurted out, "Not being able to dance and sing. I come from a place where when times are rough, or we want to celebrate something or tell an emotional story, we dance and sing. There is life and rhythm in my dancing and singing. Without it, I'm scared of what my life would be like or how I might react to all of the things I have to deal with at home, at school, on the news, you name it. I'd much rather dance and sing than be stuck in one of fear's lies."

I scribbled everything she said as fast as I could.

"Me, too," said Lauryn.

"How so, Lauryn?" asked Zack.

"I'm scared people will never learn to really like each other. My parents fight every night over money, and my older brother got beat up because he looked at someone the wrong way. He told me he was just checking out the dude's nice hat and shoes and had no idea he was dangerous. The guy confessed he thought my brother was somebody trying to jump him. It's a shame! So, for that reason, I smile because that guy could have killed my brother that day. God gave me and my brother another happier day. I smile and I dance around fear. I want people to get along and trust each other. What kind of world do we live in that we can't even check out each other's nice clothing? I won't even get into all of the stuff I've seen on the news."

"I-I like that. Smile and dance around fear." I said.

TJ jumped in and said, "I fear nothing. Fear should fear me."

"Come on TJ, we have to get through this. Be for real," said Zack.

"I mean, I guess I'm scared of makin' it."

"Huh what was that? Please explain," replied Ms. Plewitt from out of nowhere. She must've been teaching today's class with Ms. Scott; otherwise, she would've been quiet and never walked over to our group.

"I mean, I'm used to people telling me I won't make it as a rapper or go to college and stuff. Nobody made it to college in my family, and I want to go. I want to study words and spit em' to the world to change the world. I want to be a rapper, and maybe later an English or History teacher or somethin' and teach kids in a cool way. I can see myself writing rhymes to help them learn stuff."

"Interesting, TJ. Good! Let's use those feelings in today's poem," said Ms. Plewitt.

"Zack, Abigail? What do you fear?" she asked.

Zack chimed in first. "I think I fear letting my grandparents down. My parents let them down so much. My grandparents took me in when I was two years old because my parents were involved in something with the law. Now, they expect me to be so perfect. Sometimes I feel like doing something off the wall to show them that I'm just me. I want to program sound effects, music, video games, and audio visuals for movies and performers one day. Not be some genius doctor, chemist, or engineer. They always talk about how I'm so good at Math and Science. A couple of weeks ago they asked me if I wanted to go visit a top engineering college in Rolla, Missouri this summer. I'm only in the eighth grade!"

"That's what's up Zack! We need to get together and do some beat work," said TJ.

My heart seemed to beat my mouth.

"What a dynamic group! I like the way everyone is telling their truths. This is brave. This is courageous," said Ms. Plewitt.

"Abigail? What's your fear?" she asked.

I looked at her and thought about the soothing words and compliments she'd given me in yesterday's therapy session. She winked and nodded at me to give me encouragement and the approval to tell my truth.

"I-I think I'm scared of being different."

The whole group perked up and looked at me like a squirrel who just spotted a nut.

"Why?" asked Lauryn. "We're all different."

"Different is good," said Zack.

I felt an angel and a devil sitting on my right and left shoulder. The angel told me to tell the truth to be free, and the devil told me not to say anything more and remain stuck in fear. What's the worst that can happen to me? I was going to go for it! Something told me that I should try to trust my group and be honest with them.

"I-I mean because I stutter. It's hard to be heard. It's hard to feel normal," I explained.

A harmonic sequence of "awe, we hear you," "we don't mind that you stutter," and "you shouldn't feel like that" filled the spaces between us.

The balloon in my belly popped. I immediately felt good about letting the truth all the way out.

Ms. Plewitt looked like she was about to cry, but I could tell she was praising me for what I had just done.

I felt weird but better for contributing ideas to today's group poem. I barely stuttered while telling my truth.

"This is the sound of fear leaving the a-atmosphere," I started.

"This is courage drawing us near," said Lauryn.

"This is fear taking a seat in the rear," said TJ.

"This is bravery claiming its stake," said Imani.

"This is fear not winning through the mistakes we make," said Ms. Scott as she joined us.

"This is a risk I'm willing to take," said Zack.

"This is me drifting and not being afraid of letting my feet touch the ground," said Ms. Plewitt.

"This is me getting to face fear and dance all around," said Imani.

"This is me turning that fearful face and frown upside down," said Lauryn.

"This is me remixing fear to a better sound," said TJ

"This is me being okay with leaving a stutter in your ear," I said.

"I love this sound," said TJ

"This is fear leaving the atmosphere," I said

"That was fire!" exclaimed TJ. "But who wrote that down?"

"Nobody!" said Lauryn.

"I did!" said Ms. Plewitt. "I didn't want to interrupt, so I got it all down on paper for you. I will type it up and email it to Ms. Scott tonight. "Way to go team IL Beatz!"

"How did you all come up with that group name anyway?"

TJ responded, "IL should be ILL...like sick, which is slang for real good...but 'I' stands for Imani, 'L' and 'BE' stands for Lauryn Beals (her first and last name), and 'A' stands for Abigail, 'T' for TJ, and 'Z' for Zack.

"Ooooh. I love it!"

"TJ, you know that name was all about you and your rap skills," joked Imani.

"I didn't know you all still use, 'ill' or 'sick' in your generation. We totally used that in my generation," said Ms. Plewitt.

"We really don't. I just had to make it as cool as possible with the letters I had to work with," replied TJ.

"Well you all make a nice team, and I am excited to see where all of your creativity put together will take you this quarter in the Performing Arts show!" said Ms. Scott as she gave us our exit slip and dismissed class.

"Class, your exit slip is to turn in your poem or tell me Ms. Plewitt is going to email it to me. Your entry ticket for next week is to write a poetic letter to your biggest fear. Include creativity and adventure. See you next week and have a safe weekend. I have to get to this data team meeting, and we're running a little behind time."

I felt like some of my fear really left me. I was glad that I didn't let all of the stuttering from last week's class keep me from speaking up. I had so much fun with my group. If our poem was going to be like that at the Performing Arts show, then I didn't have anything to worry about.

CHAPTER 30

#BETTER TOGETHER

I was just in time for the data team meeting. Everyone was already in their collaboration nation groups. "Ms. Plewitt, over here," Ms. Scott waved to get my attention. "We rocked it in my class today!" commented Ms. Scott.

"No. You rocked it Ms. Scott. You are so passionate about what you teach. You make your students believe in magic! You even managed to bring out a little creativity in a square like me."

"You always had it in you, and as I told my students, 'everyone is born with a special kind of creativity that will serve the right purpose at the right time.' Just stop going against the grain."

"I guess I need to keep digging and coming to your class more often to unleash it."

"Now, let's talk about that mature, perfect bed of roses group of students you have this year."

"Girl, that's only my last hour. I really lucked out. Now the other periods make me nervous. I've had to deal with fights, inappropriate poetry, stealing, kids talking while I'm teaching, and students blatantly refusing to do my assignments. My last hour is a blessing I look forward to every Wednesday and Friday."

"Well I'm sorry to hear things aren't the best all day for you. I think you are doing a fantastic job! You bring life to those kids. You get them to open up and go deep within themselves. I really thought I would hear students talk about fearing bees, spiders, losing, snakes, heights, and simple stuff. But you got your students to tap into a deeper reality. Deeper fears. That's pretty amazing."

"I wasn't too surprised. This generation of students value their voice and want to be able to freely express themselves. They aren't afraid to be loud where we adults tiptoe around. They aren't afraid to tell their truths, because many of them never get the opportunity to do so. Creativity gives them that moment in time."

"Do you really think she would have done that if you weren't there or her classmates weren't so open and honest about their own fears, Ms. Plewitt? Let's not forget the popular phrase 'teamwork makes the dream work.' We are better together," Ms. Scott declared while giving me a high five.

"Speaking of teamwork," Mr. Bee interrupted as he walked to our table. "Why don't you ladies join Mrs. Bee, Mrs. Schivers, Coach Smith (the PE teacher), and Mrs. Genius (the Art teacher) in their discussion about the Fall Performing Arts Show?"

"Sure thing!" Ms. Scott and I replied at the same time.

"He sure knows how to cut our good conversations short," said Ms. Scott.

We continued talking while we moved to their table. "I was saying, speaking of teamwork, how would you feel if I shared some of the benchmarks or steps Abigail and I are taking to reach her goal of accepting stuttering and getting others to accept it with you so we both can work on it simultaneously? She used one of your poetry assignments in her journal, and it was phenomenal! It was like reading a case history or background information in a fun way. I want her to keep the rhythm going in her journal. It's definitely helping her chip away at her iceberg. I can see it helping her come out of her shell this year too."

"Ms. Plewitt, now you know you didn't even have to ask!"

"Thank you so much! One last favor. I'm scheduling her IEP meeting for two weeks from today. Will you agree to be a part of it and talk about Abigail's strengths and steps to work towards? I'm thinking about inviting the Art or Music teacher, too. Please, pretty please? I will buy you lunch!"

"Ms. Plewitt, say no more. Of course, I'll come, and maybe we can treat each other and go out to lunch or do a girl's day at the spa to refuel our creative juices one weekend. Thirty minutes isn't enough time to scarf down a decent meal anyway!"

CHAPTER 31

#BEEYOUTIFUL

"How does a supermodel slash songstress slash fashion mogul slash beauty queen arrive at being a Music teacher?" I asked Ms. Scott.

"I know, right! Ms. Bee is the most beautiful teacher inside and out," said Mrs. Schivers.

"Well, you know she always says she has a love for kids she can't quite put into words," Coach Smith chimed in.

Mrs. Bee fixed her mustard yellow silk blouse into place after she took off her light gray, cashmere wool cardigan. Her matching gray and yellow plaid pencil skirt and suede open-toe booties made me want to hit up the nearest mall after school. She even moved around gracefully, I thought.

The group became quiet. "Good Friday afternoon. Thank you so much for agreeing to meet with me to discuss the annual Fall Performing Arts Show that's only six short weeks away. We had to bump it up a few weeks this year because of the renovations our auditorium will be undergoing."

I thought someone was testing my Speech and Language limits! Did Mrs. Bee think I looked like a magician? I didn't have that many tricks up my sleeve!

"I do understand this is short notice and it may seem like it's impossible to put a show together so quickly, but that's why I wanted to talk to all of you about coming up with a more creative theme this year. We don't have to do our usual show-stopping concert. I'm envisioning a symbolic theme. One that tells a story. One that symbolizes what our middle school students have evolved into and the roles they are stepping into."

"You mean a rite of passage?" asked Mrs. Schivers.

"Not exactly, but very similar. I want us to ask our students to showcase how they have used their talents and gifts to overcome things of this world."

"Yeah, you know St. Louis has been through it, and our students have been so strong. We have to paint a brighter picture of the future for our students," said Mrs. Genius.

"Yes. Exactly! I want them to look beyond the audience, their family, friends, and surroundings. I want them to find the one thing that makes them unique and sets their hearts on fire. Whether it be dancing like nobody's watching, singing like their voices will open the sky, painting a portrait with no boundaries or instructions, playing an instrument like it's their most powerful gift in life to the beat of a song never sang, or reciting poetry that shakes the nation. I want them to realize that they are the instruments created to shine!"

"Are you saying you want to give the students free range to decide how and what they will do?" Ms. Scott asked.

"Absolutely."

"That is perfect! I'm teaching a poetry unit this quarter, so I got you covered there."

"Thank you, Ms. Scott," said Mrs. Bee.

"I have quite a few painters and artists who could either work on props or the background or paint during a performance. Like they do at church," said Mrs. Genius.

"I love that idea. I will be working with those who want to sing, rap, or play instruments," commented Mrs. Bee.

"I can work with the cheer and dance teams during after school practices," said Coach Smith.

"See, it's all coming together already! I have a feeling this will be our best show yet!" exclaimed Mrs. Bee.

"Ms. Plewitt and Mrs. Schivers, will you assist wherever possible to encourage students and help build their confidence in believing in themselves? I would hate for any student to back out because they feel they can't do it."

"No problem. We'd be happy to," said Mrs. Schivers.

"I'm thinking I need to focus on Abigail," I whispered to Mrs. Schivers.

"Remember, the Lord always provides. Trust Him to use you exactly where He needs you. Maybe He wants you to take a step back and watch Him perform His marvelous works. Have faith in His waves! Let God get the glory!" ended Mrs. Schivers.

I clasped my hands together and thanked Mrs. Schivers for her beautiful and powerful words.

"Mrs. Bee. I got it," I raised my hand. "We could call the show Being YOU!"

"Fantastic!"

"We will start rehearsal next Friday. Until then, spend some time exploring with your students. Collaborate with other teachers in the building as well. I will email a sign-up sheet for performance slots. The elementary music teacher is in charge of their portion of the show, so I have a great feeling we will be just fine and on time!"

CHAPTER 32

#STEP INTO THE LIGHT

I thought about how I would write a letter to my biggest fear. I didn't understand the reason for all the crazy writing assignments. It was obvious the assignments and my journal entries started to overlap. I could bet money that Ms. Scott and Ms. Plewitt hung out with each other after school. They probably planned all their assignments and lessons together while keeping me at the center of their thoughts. Stuttering was my biggest fear, but my fear of everyone hearing me stutter might have been bigger.

I knew the students in my focus group said they didn't care that I stuttered, but what about everyone else? Still, so many people didn't know much about it, nor did they know me. All I knew was that I stuttered. Mr. Bee once announced something about the fear of the unknown. Avoiding it only keeps us where we are. I no longer wanted to see eye-to-eye with fear, and I didn't want it stealing any more of my

155

sparkle. It's time to work on dimming my fear of stuttering's light forever!

Dear Stutter,

This is my light. Not yours! I'm coming out of your shell. I'm stepping into my light. You can memorize and meditate on that!

This isn't my actual letter to fear but it's a start.

❤ Abigail Brewer

CHAPTER 33

#FEAR FACTOR CHALLENGE NO.1: ISABELLE'S SPELL

"Girls, get dressed. Get your shoes on and grab your jackets. It's Saturday night and you know that means your Granny ain't cookin'! We're going out for dinner!" yelled Papa.

"Where are we going?" asked Natalia.

"I was thinking a buffet so you all can get exactly what you want."

"The China Buffet?" I suggested.

"Ewww gross. Nobody wants Chinese all of the time. You are the only person I know who always wants Chinese or Mexican food," snarled Isabelle.

157

"Isabelle stop talking to your sister like that! I know of a place that has all you can eat choices of Mexican, Chinese, American, Greek, Italian, and SEEfood. Meaning anything you see you can eat it! So, let's all load on up in Suzy-Q."

"Sorry Papa," said Isabelle.

I rolled my eyes at Isabelle because she knew she should've apologized to me. She flinched at me like she was going to hit me or something. She was always a whole lot of talk and no show, so I wasn't worried at all about her. It's on and poppin', and I felt like pouncing if she made fun of my stutter again.

We arrived at the restaurant. We waited thirty minutes for a table.

"I forgot senior citizens eat free on Saturday nights. It'll be worth the wait, girls. I promise." Papa assured us as we stood in line twirling our thumbs, people watching, and repositioning our bodies to a more comfortable position every few minutes.

Isabelle started humming and singing and drawing attention to us. It's obviously the wrong place and time for this because the room was filled with seniors. Papa even asked her to keep it down. She listened for a few minutes before she continued. Then did it again and again and again.

Was she in her own world? How and why did she disrespect Papa in public? Granny would've yanked her outside and set her straight. I decided to try to help Papa with her.

"I-I-Isabelle. Papa said be q-quiet."

"You shut up you stuttering mutt!" said Isabelle.

I had to ask the Lord for forgiveness for the actions that were about to take place!

The waitress seated us and told us to help ourselves to the buffet.

I let Isabelle go ahead of me to fix her plate. I piled a nice helping of Chinese fried rice, lo-mein, orange chicken, Spanish rice, and Mexican queso and tortilla chips all on one plate. I drenched the food in salsa, guacamole, and sour cream. It looked like a plate full of slop. Isabelle made an abrupt stop, and I accidentally bumped into her. Some of my food smeared on my lettermen cheer jacket.

"E-E-E-Excuse you!" Isabelle turned around and mocked my stutter again.

Before I could even blink or think of something to say, I tipped my plate up and shoved it all in her face and yelled, "Now who's the mutt!"

I kept yelling at her as I pushed her to the ground and wrestled with her. "I'm so sick of you thinking you can say whatever you want, talk about me, and make fun of my stuttering! You aren't better than anybody around here, and the next time you think you're going to bully me I will make you choke and stutter on your own words!"

Isabelle looked at me, cried, and stuttered, "Get-get off me," and ran to the restaurant bathroom. I saw the smirk on Natalia and Papa's faces as they backed away from trying to get me off of Isabelle.

We were kicked out of the restaurant, and Isabelle was forced to apologize and promise that she would never tease or bully me again.

That's how it happened in my mind; you should know me better than that by now.

You might be shocked when you read what happened, or should I say how who had to be an angel sent from heaven stepped in and handled the situation.

When I bumped into Isabelle and she mocked my stuttering, an older lady heard her, turned around, and told her how she grew up stuttering and that her niece and nephew also stutter. She told Isabelle it was okay to stutter, and she was going to have to learn to be confident when she speaks more than anything else. The lady thought Isabelle stuttered!

Furthermore, she said, "What you have to say is far more important than worrying about stuttering while you say it. Let your voice be heard! I had to learn this the hard way growing up. I barely talked to anybody because I was afraid of being made fun of. Those people who think it's okay to make fun of stuttering and other differences in people might want to think about the idea behind God being creative in ALL His works. The Bible says, "I praise you because I am fearfully and wonderfully made; your works are wonderful, I know that full well."

(Psalm 139:14, NIV). I want you to know full well that you are perfect just the way you are. You are wonderful because His works are wonderful! In fact, I bet He placed you right here, right now, with me to deliver this message. Stutter openly, stutter confidently, and watch all the negative people and negative energies disappear into thin air. Watch those chains start breaking! And watch your little light become magnified in His purpose for you! Look at your light from different angles. Look at everything that shines in you."

She looked at both of us and said, "And lastly, watch the evil little spell of a bully break completely away from you."

I didn't know which part of the woman's confession struck Isabelle like lightning, but she didn't bother me after she heard it. I didn't have to say a word. I only hoped it would last.

My mixed plate of food tasted better as I meditated on those wise words during dinner.

I silently praised the Lord that I am fearfully and wonderfully made. I no longer felt so ashamed of His wonderful works. I guess He has marvelous ideas behind my stutter.

Ms. Plewitt,

This Saturday I met an older lady who stuttered. She said she also has a niece and nephew who stutter. I wish I could meet them, but it was nice to finally meet someone else who stutters. Isabelle teased and mocked me for stuttering again and this lady just so happened to hear her mocking me. She thought Isabelle was the one who stutters and gave us some really good advice. I think she may have even cracked Isabelle's devilish shell, but time will tell! The thing that stood out the most was a scripture she quoted from the Bible. "I am fearfully and wonderfully made." I feel bad that I have been making my stutter so much bigger than the creative works behind my creation. I AM so much more than a stutter!

I AM

The special piece of His masterplan

The perfect fit to a puzzle

I AM

A sun-kissed goddess with chestnut eyes and golden-brown hair

A drop of sweetness in His air

I AM

The speed of light on a track

The balance on a beam who flips back

I AM

The artist that draws us close

The poet aspiring to reach cosmos

I Am

The marvel in His creation

The beautiful speck in my diamond

I AM

The command of His light

The shiny in His bright

I AM

A friend

A sister

A daughter

I AM

A Person who stutters

The importance of the ship's rudders

I Am

The miracle in the rod

I Am

A child of God

I Am

Not afraid

For I Am

Fearfully and wonderfully made!

CHAPTER 34

#DEAR GOLIATH

"Come on, girls. We are so late for church. I'm gonna miss worship and get terrible seats in the pew. Whew, Lord, help us get there before Pastor Daily starts preachin'! I can't walk in late. Sister Iralee will talk all about me," Granny said as she wiped and blotted sweat from her forehead and chin with her thick red makeup sponge that smelled like Oil of Olay.

Granny's voice rattled, as she fussed and cursed every time we were running late. She was from whom I learned to be early or on time for everything. I broke out in a nervous sweat from listening to her. None of us could grab our stuff and jump in Suzy-Q fast enough.

Papa skirted out of the driveway and made sharp turns around every corner. I was positive we were on two wheels a few times. I was so scared that I felt my palms soak the sticky note revealing my Goliath. I glanced over at Natalia's note, but I couldn't read her tiny cursive handwriting. I looked at Isabelle's chicken scratch; it read, "Failing is my Goliath."

I didn't know why she was worried about failing. I've never seen her report cards, but I thought she performed okay in school. She's good at dancing, and her singing wasn't terrible. What was she talking about?

We walked into the church, where the entire congregation stood and stretched their arms up to Heaven as if they were reaching for Jesus' hands. One of the lead worship singers was on her knees singing the song about breaking chains by Tasha Cobbs-Leonard. I couldn't help but to start singing along before we sat down. I kept singing as Granny found seats at the front that sister Iralee saved for us.

We filed in and kept singing. I didn't know why, but I developed an emotional attachment to that song. For the first time I was in tears singing it with the others. It's like I felt and heard some of the chains that held my feelings about stuttering breaking. Isabelle, Granny, Papa, and Mama were in tears, too. I didn't know Isabelle could cry. Mama was probably praying for the chains to break off her money so we could live in a new house. Granny and Papa were probably praying for the same thing. Natalia was in awe, recording the performance because a violinist was playing during the song.

Pastor Daily walked on the stage and declared, "I hear so many chains being broken in the whole congregation today. Everybody shout 'Amen!' if you hear them as well. Shout 'Amen' if you see this army rising up all around you to break every chain."

He slowed his speech to match the slowing rhythm of the song. "You see that army isn't just all of us. There is a greater magnitude. If we're the army then God is our Commander in Chief, and He promised us that 'No weapon formed against you shall prosper.' (Isaiah 54:17, NKJV, abbreviated). Oh, I feel like giving you a full meal before I even get to what I planned to serve you today," he preached.

"You see, you are a part of God's army, and He will not let you be defeated. Stop believing the enemies lies. Tweens and teens, stop letting the haters bring you down with their words."

Pastor blotted his forehead with his rag as he paced the stage in his new shoes. He was always so cool with his wardrobe. I thought, like me, he must have a sneaker fetish.

"Furthermore, God equips His army with the full armor of God to win any battle thrown their way. And I'm here to tell you that you better put it on! In Ephesians 6:11, NIV, God tells us to 'put on the whole armor of God, so that you can take your stand against the devil's schemes.' Yes, they are schemes to keep you from the victories he knows that God promised you in your future. That armor is your victory! Everybody in the pews better believe that you ain't too young, too old, too broke, too rich, too pretty, or too different to put on God's armor. And I'm not done telling y'all what all His perfect armor entails."

The Pastor took a deep breath and explained all the armors God has given us to put on at all times like prayer, faith, truth, righteousness, peace, salvation, the Word, and prayer. Pastor continued, "Notice I said

ALL TIMES and not SOMETIMES. That means kids you can wear this armor to school, to sports practice and games, to camp, to dinner, to hang out with yo friends, to the corner store, at home, when you do homework, when you interact with your siblings, even when you washin' yo stanky behind! Because the enemy is real. And his only job is to kill, steal, and destroy. Wear your full armor!"

"Amen!" everyone shouted.

Pastor had me daydreaming about victory over my fears of stuttering. I started to picture myself as an adventurous teenage warrior using all the mighty spiritual weapons and armors to defeat and break the chains of fear and stuttering. I snapped back into the sermon.

"Youngsters in the buildin', what armor are you using to fight your daily battles? Are ya' carrying the wrong armor that causes somebody else's chains of hurt, bullying, teasing, heartache, disappointment, fear, or jealousy? If so, it's never too late to switch out your armor!"

Pastor ran down the steps onto the bright red carpet and said, "I veered way off from the sermon I originally wrote, but the Lord told me all of y'all needed to be reminded of the armor God graciously gifted you with. That armor will help you so much in this world. So, I don't usually do this, but I'm gonna get to the point with David and Goliath because I have something special for this nice lil' army of tweens and teens today!"

"Touch your neighbor and say I'm ready for my Pastor Daily's bread."

Isabelle and Natalia touched me and repeated after Pastor. For once, Isabelle flashed a believable smile at me. The Lord must've broken her chains of being so cruel at times!

About 15 of the ninth through twelfth-grade Higher Calling youth group members wheeled a giant cross to the front of the church and laid it flat on the floor.

"I-I hope pastor doesn't have us c-come stomp on the c-c-cross like he did those M&M's last week!" I said to Natalia.

"I know, right. That would hurt," she replied.

We looked at the Pastor as he began speaking. "Now I don't have the time I need to go all into the story of David and Goliath, but here is what I want you to know. I also want you to go home and study it with your family and friends."

He paused and sat on the first step facing our section of the pews and began to summarize it.

"The story begins in the first book of Samuel in the Bible."

As Pastor continued, I began thinking about my assignment to write a letter to fear. After hearing Pastor's summary I was inspired. I knew exactly what I was going to say to my Goliath in my letter. Just as David was anointed and chosen by God for kingship because of all the good things God saw on the inside of him, I felt like God probably gave me the journal and poetry assignments because He saw my heart. He probably knew I wanted to slay my fears once and for all and I'd seek Him and depend on Him to do it. I felt like I was probably being equipped with all the armor I needed. Maybe all of my teachers, Ms. Plewitt, my focus group members, friends, family, classes, and journal entries were all part of my training. Sort of like David's first job of tending the sheep in the field. During his job he fought off and killed lions and bears with his bare hands when they came near the sheep. He trained with pebbles and a slingshot in his spare time. It prepared him to do the greatest thing ever that no one else had the courage to even attempt to do. No one even thought he was qualified to do it. He defeated Goliath! Goliath was a giant undefeated champion that was six cubits in height and armed with all kinds of bronze and a big ole' spear that everybody was scared of. Nobody wanted to face this giant. But young and inexperienced, scrawny, teenage David said and believed that the same Lord that saved him from the lions and bears will save him from Goliath and He did. He took Goliath out with one stone, one sling, one shot, and with one thing from God - His armor! He trusted God's armor!

Suddenly I felt empowered. Perhaps my words or my performance will be my stone that defeats my Goliath.

Pastor encouraged and reminded us we're never too young for a kingdom assignment from God! We're never chosen based on our outer appearance or excluded because we don't look or seem like we fit for the part. God doesn't call the equipped; He equips the called. He emphasized, God looks at our hearts. So it doesn't matter if we don't speak the best, have all the experience we need, or if we feel we don't measure up in our eyes because God has a different set of lenses and He sees what's on the inside of everyone!

I focused in on Pastor again when I heard him say, "So, this is the icing on the cake. Mmmm. That sounds so good. Jilly's Cupcake and Ice Cream Bar, here I come after this sermon. You better have my Bee Sting and Twisted Pink Velvet cupcakes waitin' on me! Okay, I'm running over time but stick with me and meet me at the cupcake bar after the sermon okay."

Pastor laughed.

"Now I want all the tweens and teens to come to the front of this cross, bring your Goliath's and give them to me. I know there's at least 20 or 30 of ya, but just circle around this cross for me."

The Pastor dropped our Goliath's in a bucket.

"Now I want one of you to pick up this giant cross and set it upwards."

He held the mic to a boy who said, "I can't."

"Why not? You've got His coat of armor and His army right in front of ya'. Use your faith and trust in His armor!" said Pastor Daily.

The boy asked all of us to help. We quickly figured out how to roll it upright. It stood about 10 feet high.

"I bet you didn't know how giant it was when it was laying down did ya? You see, God knew you would need help, so he sent an army of all of these people around you to help you. He didn't want you to believe the lie that 'you can't do it!' Let me tell you somethin'. You can do all things through Christ who strengthens you! (Philippians, 4:13, NKJV, abbreviated, emphasis added). And you can do all things with the army and armor God gave you! You gotta' just tell everybody including yourself 'You can and will do it' and shout out the only tools you need. Ask and you shall receive!"

"Now, now, now, wait a minute. One last thing. I want all of you to reach in this bucket and grab a Goliath. I know you might not grab yours, but guess what: it was NEVER yours! Christ died on that cross to defeat that Goliath for you as long as you call on Him! Wooooooo! Somebody give me an Amen!"

"Now to close this up before benediction, I want all of you to nail the Goliath you grabbed to this cross and leave it there for Jesus to carry and help you defeat. Do it now! Remember it was never yours! Give it to Christ!"

With that, the congregation did about everything but cartwheels!

It felt so good to leave my Goliath of fear because of my stutter at the cross. I had all the tools I need to face that Goliath!

I was going to complete Ms. Scott's assignment in my journal and on separate piece of paper because I want Ms. Plewitt to see it too.

Dear Goliath,

Should I address you by your proper name of Fear, middle name of Stuttering, and last name Defeated?

Oh wait, you thought no one would read it.

You wanted me to refer to you as a deep seeded secret.

You wanted me to make you seem bigger than the only one we all fear...

The Lord Jesus Christ who loves me dear, and who I keep near!

Goliath!

You're close. I give you that. You're lurking. I know it. You're searching. I see.

For the perfect opportunity to seize little ole' me.

Goliath!

Why don't you pick on somebody your own size?

Oh wait, that person isn't just any old person.

He's in a disguise

that only those who have faith can see with their eyes.

His height is infinite cubics, and His stature is stronger than steel.

His helmet is brighter than the sun, His right hand is accompanied by His son.

In Him lies peace and honor.

In His house in Heaven, His will be done.

Goliath!

Fear!

You've been confronted by a Holy one.

Stuttering you can stay. But on this day. I came to slay.

Goliath!

Fear!

Maybe you should run and hide.

Oh wait, I forgot about your armor of pride.

Goliath!

Maybe you should step aside or take a seat.

Oh wait, I forgot about the heavy metal armor of arrogance shackled to your feet.

Goliath!

Maybe you should turn around.

Oh wait, I forgot your armor doesn't trust what you can't see.

Goliath!

Maybe you should just leave.

Oh wait, I forgot about the armor of bondage you carry on your sleeve.

Goliath!

I gave you the opportunity to go.

But, oh wait, I forgot there's this other thing you don't know.

Part of that person that isn't just any old person resides in me.

He has equipped me with so much victory that I don't even care if you live.

You see He's given me the armor of His courage, the armor of His strength, and the armor of His bravery.

Goliath!

Fear!

Welcome! You are now captive in my slavery!

You serve me. And I serve God.

And while you were too busy – trying to be so scary,

I broke your chains and cuffed your feet to God's mighty sanctuary.

Goliath!

One move and you will fall.

A giant fall.

But don't worry. God will get the glory.

Once and for all!

♥ Abigail Brewer

CHAPTER 35

#SWEETS FOR THE SWEET

"Jilly's actually sounds pretty good right now," said Papa. Papa was what we call a sugar addict in our house. Every time we turned around, he's munching on jelly beans, peanuts, Swedish Fish jelly candies, ice cream, cookies, cake, you name it. Granny always pinched off a bit of whatever he had because she's diabetic and she constantly talked about watching her sugar.

"I'm treating Papa's angels today! Gone ahead to the bathroom and wash your hands. I'll stand in line so we don't have to wait long," said Papa.

The line began to extend out the front door of the restaurant. Pastor Daily must have put the same mouth-watering sweet tooth in everyone's mouth during his sermon. It was funny that I didn't see Pastor Daily or First Lady there, though.

I went into the bathroom with Isabelle and Natalia. I looked up in the big mirror above the sink that was framed with a pink, ice-glazed painted frame when I finished washing my hands. I noticed Isabelle's reflection of what looked to be a sullen face. I felt like she might be nice to me after all of the stuff that happened this weekend, and the sermon through which we just sat through that pretty much spelled out DON'T BE THE CAUSE OF ANYONE ELSE'S GOLIATH. I hoped she took that to heart and finally wised up on the fact that God armored me to be victorious over people who treated me like she did. I asked her, "Are you okay? You look sad."

To my surprise, she broke down and cried. I just knew she was going apologize to me and give me a big hug so we could live happily ever after. Not so much!

"I keep getting D's and F's on my fourth hour class assignments, and I'm scared to tell Mama, Papa, and Granny. I know they will find out on my progress report in a couple weeks and take me out of dance until I get my grades up. Ms. Scott gave me one week to turn in some poems for extra credit. She told me to stay after school, but I have so much other homework that I can't," cried Isabelle.

By this time her tears became waterfalls that drowned out the flushing sounds in the stalls. Her eyes were getting red and puffy. She looked so pitiful. I had to do something to help her. I wet some paper towels and helped her get her snot-nose face back together.

She continued, "Ms. Scott suggested that you might be able to help me, but, but, but," she stuttered.

She started crying hard again.

"But what?" I asked as I wiped her face again.

She couldn't bring herself to ask me.

"I-Isabelle, of c-course I will help you. We can start tonight," I responded and hugged her. She sniffled, sniffed, sighed, and eventually calmed down.

"Thanks. You're so sweet. How do you do it Abigail? You're so kind and good at everything."

Those sweet words were like chocolate lava oozing out of my heart. They instantly made me forget about everything she had done to me. I guess I have plenty of the fruit of forgiveness in my shell.

Isabelle finished pulling herself together and we walked out of the bathroom.

Pastor Daily turned the corner to the hall leading to the restrooms and yelled, "Twins! Hey, how y'all doin'? You two have been on my mind since my M and Ms sermon, and I just have to tell ya that God is so good and working in y'all's lives. And I wanna leave y'all with a sweet ole' scripture the good Lord whispered to me on the way here."

This time, the Pastor looked directly at me and said, "People think you're quiet, but your voice is one of the loudest in the room when it comes to showing others the heart of Christ. Don't ever shy away from that. Just remember this scripture for me. 'For God gave us not a spirit of fear but of power and love and self-control.'" (2 Timothy 1:7, ESV, abbreviated).

All I could do was thank Pastor Daily for his daily dessert.

I don't know why I felt like he continues preaching directly to me. Whatever he was doing was surely helping me to stop hiding in my shell because of my stutter.

CHAPTER 36

#SIGNS

"**G**ood Monday Morning and welcome to the hood on this glorious day. I have quite a few announcements this morning, so Beeeee patient with me. I wouldn't want the head dragons to have to blow any steam. I'm sure that would cause a pretty big fire around here."

Mr. Bee was very corny, and it was too early for this. I needed to talk to Abigail's teacher to remind her about the IEP meeting I scheduled for next week.

"First, as you all know, Mrs. Bee is hosting the annual Fall Performing Arts Show. It will take place exactly 6 weeks from today on the evening of Friday, October 12th. I know this is a lot sooner than all of you fellow dragons anticipated but, as Aristotle once said, '*There is no great genius without some touch of madness.*' While it may seem that such a short time to prepare will drive us dragons into chaos, we must remember to take our time and value the time we are given. For Aristotle also said,

'*Patience is bitter, but its fruit is sweet,*' so we are all going to soar gracefully through this to showcase the fruit of all of our magical genius' here at Robinhood."

I wondered if he wrote down those quotes. The clock was about 20 minutes from alerting me to pick up my first group of the day when I heard the swish sound of Abigail's journal slide under my door. I tuned out the rest of the announcements and prayed before I opened it.

"Lord, I'm starting to see that you are guiding me through everything I do with Abigail this year. I thank you for your tools of textbooks, encouraging coworkers, and putting specific teachers in my army to help me do what you've asked me to do. Mostly I thank you for allowing me to rely on your full coat of armor to support her where she needs it most. I trust you and I believe you. Please continue to show me your mighty and perfect works. Amen."

I opened the journal and felt a strange, quickening sensation in my heart. I felt goosebumps as I read Dear Goliath and her other recent entries.

"Lord, you are so good to me!" I have absolutely nothing to fear this year!" I continued in prayer. "Thank you for these signs! Please keep helping me help Abigail find adventure in all of this. Help me to help her use all the tools you've equipped her with, and all the people you've surrounded her with, such as Ms. Scott and everyone else around her, to allow her to smooth out her speech to a rhythm that's perfect to you Lord."

CHAPTER 37

#THE COUNTDOWN

" Alright class. Today, we are jumping right in to discuss the Fall Performing Arts Show Poetry segment."

Ms. Scott's face was carrying a different tune today.

"This year, Mrs. Bee would like you to tell your story. Tell the story you've been daring to share with the world. Be bold. Be courageous. Be brave. Be YOU!" Ms. Scott paused, read the room, and took a deep breath in and exhaled on a big profound grin.

"And remember...May every parent's heart remember the reason for your season. Make every audience member settle in their seat and tune their antennas into your unexpected beat. Let the beat of your drum turn you numb to the crowd's unknown outcome. Let the swirls and twirls of the dance you do with your words set you free to sing like a mockingbird. And remember through this spoken word: it's your voice waiting to be heard!"

Snaps and claps filled the air.

Ms. Scott finished with, "The only rules are to work together and let everyone's light shine!"

We broke into our focus groups and immediately began talking about different things we've never told anybody, laughed about our most embarrassing moments, and things we were frustrated with at school and in our community. We talked about guns, racism, not enough teachers in the building, the rich, the poor, politics, parents, money, terrorism, divided nations, God, and bullying. We had so much to say that we didn't make any progress. Everybody did, however, discover that I was a pretty good poet because Ms. Scott walked to our table and shared some exciting news with me.

"Abigail, I almost forgot to thank you for helping one of my students. Let me be the first to tell you that the three assignments the student turned in were all A+ papers. You should be very proud of yourself. It takes a lot to help someone else be successful in something that they don't quite believe is one of their strengths!"

I knew she was trying to be discreet because she didn't want my group to know she's talking about my twin sister Isabelle.

"Th-thank you Ms. Scott."

"Aha! That's what she meant by that statement she made the first week of school. We have to totally work with Abigail to fit all of our ideas, including her own, into this epic poem that makes the whole room shake," said TJ

"TJ, you might be onto something," said Imani.

"Tell me more," said Lauryn.

"I mean. Like we all have these crazy good ideas and deep stories to tell. I just think we need to make sure we tell it well," responded TJ.

"I like that, TJ. I can see visuals and everything," said Zack.

"I can see dance and movement and bits of singing," said Imani.

"I can see us including everyone," said Lauryn.

"I can see the hook being echoed with my drums," said TJ.

"A-and what do you all see me doing?" I asked.

"Duh! Reciting it!" joked Lauryn.

"It's really hard for someone else to recite someone else's poetry to the same rhythm they wrote it in. It just doesn't sound as sincere," said Imani.

"Umm. Don't you all remember I stutter?"

"Girl, who cares! I mean sorry if that sounded harsh, but your poetry must be on point for Ms. Scott to come over here bragging like that. How about we all give you our ideas, you write something, we'll read it next week, and then decide if we all recite it together or whatever," said Lauryn.

"We got you, Abigail," said TJ

"Yeah, we have your back. In my culture, we first feel our story, then connect it to the sounds in our mind, we begin shuffling, scuffling, and stomping, then we match the beats of our heart and movements of our feet to the music. We sing and we dance to the rhythm of our story. I think you will find a rhythm to the story once you write it. You have to speak to that rhythm when you recite it," said Imani.

"Aww," Snap, snap, snap. "That was so beautiful," said Lauryn.

"O-okay fine!" I felt so much pressure for the rest of the period. My group really believed in me. I didn't want to let them down. I thought I could record it because I didn't stutter when I was reading or speaking alone. That way, I could lip sync at the show. Who was I kidding? My school didn't have that kind of technology. I prayed that the Lord would bring me back to trusting big, depending on His armor, and giving me the tools I needed to make it through.

CHAPTER 38

#IEP (INDIVIDUALIZED EDUCATION PLAN): A.K.A INVITED EVERY PERSON ON THE PLANET

The last time I came to my IEP meeting, I didn't have to do anything but tell the group of teachers and my family that I enjoy going to speech class with Ms. Plewitt and that I thought I was getting better. On this day, Ms. Plewitt wanted me to tell the group my goals, the tools I was using that year, and what's going well and not so well. That's a lot of talking. Did Ms. Plewitt plan to say nothing? The good news was if my mom came, she would talk everyone's ear off the whole time.

Mr. Bee, Ms. Plewitt, Mrs. Schivers, Mrs. Bee, Ms. Scott, Coach Smith, Mama, Papa, and Granny all sucked the air out the tiny conference room as the sound of squeaking rolling wheels, clanging plastic armrests, greetings, handshakes, elbows striking the tabletop, and papers crossing the hard surface of the table sent me into a state of alarm. I couldn't breathe. I didn't know what to expect, and I didn't know why all these people were there. I thought I did something wrong and was being kicked out of speech class.

Ms. Plewitt read the agenda and gave me the floor.

"Uhm. Hi e-e-everybody," I stuttered.

Everyone looked so pleasant and eager to hear what I had to say. I caught Mrs. Schivers bowing her head down for a quick prayer. That reminded me to be brave. Goliath was chained to a sanctuary, and I didn't have to let him loose.

"Ahem. Ahem. Hi," I cleared my voice to try to sound more confident.

"Thanks for c-coming," I said as I took a breath and remembered all these teachers and family members were on my side. They weren't in the business of unchaining my Goliath.

"Speech is going really good this year. I-I'm learning not to be so scared to stutter. I-I'm making new friends and they don't c--c--care that I stutter, so I'm starting to think, 'why should I?'"

They responded with gentle laughter, and Papa interrupted, "No you shouldn't baby girl. You're perfect just the way you are."

"I am learning that I have a lot of people here to help me."

That came out as smooth as a baby's bottom. I continued as goosebumps covered my arms, "My toolbox is helping me. I mean I used to think I sounded silly when I slow down, streeetch my words, pause, talk in shorter phrases, breathe easy, and then speak, so I stopped using those tools."

Ms. Plewitt's face turned red. I didn't know if she was scared because of what I'd said, or if she was sad because I felt that way.

"I'm learning it's more important to just say what I need to say, so I'm starting to trust in using my t-t-tools a-a-a-again." I rubbed my thighs and let out a gasp and continued, "My toolbox is growing, and I'm thankful I have all of you, and some pretty a-amazing friends in it. My goal is to just be o-okay with stuttering and teach other people to be okay with it too. I-I do want to find more rhythm when I speak to stutter less, but I know I will get better." I took a long pause. "Ummm, that's it," I concluded.

You could hear a pin drop in the room because it was so silent. I listened to the ticking of the second hand on the clock. Mrs. Bee leaned over, smiled, and said, "I will help you find your rhythm."

Mr. Bee sat back in his chair, rubbed his beard, and said, "whatever you need you, let me know. It's my job to make sure you get the best experiences here at Robinhood."

Granny and Papa cried tears of happiness.

Mama said, "I know my daughter, and ever since she was born God has given me a special peace about her. I know that she will achieve whatever she sets her mind to."

"Awe, thank you, Mama!" I said.

Mrs. Schivers made a few suggestions about teaching me to zone my feelings in a positive direction to regulate them before I speak – whatever that meant. Coach Smith suggested that Ms. Plewitt and I come to one of her upcoming mindfulness and yoga units of study for something to do with my breathing. Everyone provided suggestion after suggestion before Ms. Plewitt adjourned the meeting with, "Well thank you so much, Abigail, for leading us through your meeting, and it sounds like we have permission to get creative and adventurous in helping you find your rhythm!"

Ms. Scott stayed afterwards to tell my family how well I was doing in her poetry class. Mrs. Bee also told them about the Fall Performing Arts show.

That IEP wasn't so bad after all! I was glad it was out of the way. Ms. Plewitt knew she had her ways of making me talk.

CHAPTER 39

#LET THE ADVENTURES BEGIN

Over the weekend, I didn't waste any time working on the group poem. The whole group wrote some pretty serious things about which they wanted me to write. At first, I felt uncomfortable, but Ms. Scott once said, "If poetry doesn't challenge you, and you don't allow yourself to get uncomfortable, then you are limiting yourself. You aren't going deep enough. You aren't climbing high enough, and you aren't discovering the hidden treasure." I would've added my own personal touch and said, "If my poetry isn't challenging me, then I'm just skating on the iceberg, and I want to shatter the iceberg!"

I was tired of hiding behind it and worrying about how I sound, how I stutter, when I stutter, what it looks like, and feeling different and embarrassed by it. Like a freak of nature or something. I remembered what Pastor Daily said about not having a spirit if fear and being timid. I wasn't going to spend the rest of eighth grade, high school, college, and my artistic career letting fear of stuttering reign over me.

I was getting pumped, so I turned up my radio and heard a Kendrick Lamar song. I immediately thought about TJ's story of wanting to become a rapper and him feeling like he didn't know enough words to be successful. I would tell TJ to practice and study words, study other rappers, and believe in himself. Rappers are like poets. They have a story to tell behind their words. I started rapping along to his lyrics and wondered what the real story was behind his words. TJ tried to tell me that Kendrick Lamar had a story like mine, but I had no clue what he meant.

I grabbed the family laptop and searched for Kendrick Lamar.

"No way. Oh my gosh! No way! Shut up!" I exclaimed in response to what I found. Kendrick Lamar used to stutter and put all his energy into his songs to overcome it! "This is impossible! He didn't stutter when he rapped – then again, neither did I. I'm so done! This is too cool." Suddenly, I didn't feel so alone in this world.

A link to the Stuttering Foundation of America was displayed at the bottom of the page for other famous people who stutter. I clicked it and saw the following names:

Ed Sheeran (one of my favorite singers)

Tiger Woods (a famous golfer)

Derek Jeter (a former professional baseball player)

Julia Roberts (an amazing actress)

Samuel Jackson (a hilariously funny actor)

Emily Blunt (a beautiful and talented actress)

Tim Gunn (OMG! The host of that reality TV show, Project Runway..."Tim, I so want to be a fashion designer one day!")

Adrian Peterson (a famous football player)

Charles Darwin (I learned about him in an article at school)

B.B. King and Elvis Presley (Granny's favorite blues singer and the king of Rock and Roll)

So many athletes, singers, actors, actresses, kings, vice presidents, business leaders, musicians, writers, photographers, artists, composers, and even Moses from the Bible were listed. I wondered if any poets stuttered.

I entered 'Famous Poets who stutter' in the search engine. An interesting fact about a guy named Lewis Carroll popped up. He wrote Alice in Wonderland! This was becoming more interesting! A link to a story about

James Earl Jones, the original voice of Darth Vader in Star Wars was also listed! He used poetry to overcome his stutter and became an actor! He never stopped stuttering. He learned to work with it.

I thought that's what I wanted to do – learn to work with it or alongside it.

None of the famous people let stuttering stop them from shining.

I no longer could hold in all my excitement. I was far from being alone in the world because about 70 million people stutter nationwide.

I wished that I could talk to some of them. Until then, I felt like dancing. This information was music to my ears!

I stood and flung my white and gold desk chair out of the way, kicked off my emoji slippers, and broke it down. I jumped in front of the mirror, whipped my poofy ponytail back and forth, and grabbed my pencil and pretended I was rapping the Kendrick Lamar song that was playing. I must have forgotten I was pretending because I heard my voice get louder and faster when the song's hooks came.

I was all into it. I did all kinds of dances, new and old, like the milly rock, footwork, and dab, and I found myself imitating dance challenges I'd seen on YouTube.

Soon, Natalia busted in and said, "What is all of this noise? I'm trying to practice a new song on my violin!" Isabelle ran in the room and danced like she wanted to battle me.

"I-Isabelle, you really don't want to challenge me!" I said.

Natalia jumped in and said, "Bring it. I'm shutting down the both of y'all." We danced, sang, and laughed the night away. We later reminisced about old times and embarrassing moments.

We hadn't had that much fun together in forever, it seemed. And to think that may have been the last year we spent in Granny and Papa's house if God answered our prayers of finding a new home by the end of the school year.

CHAPTER 40

#CREATIVE JUICES

The next few weeks at school felt like I was preparing for a big role in a movie production like actors and actresses do. I didn't have to learn martial arts, Jiu-jitsu, or how to speak a foreign language, but I did get to focus on letting my creativity flow. I was putting my everything into it.

Ms. Plewitt visited all my classes at least twice. The teachers should've added her name to the roll. In my English class, she helped me practice choral reading excerpts from stories with the class, and encouraged me to volunteer to speak and read aloud in front of the class more. I didn't know that I stuttered less when I began reading with others then tune the other readers out, so my voice was the only one I heard. It's like I needed a little push to get off the ground and get used to the rhythm before I took off reading by myself.

I didn't get to dodge Mr. Bee's quests in Science class. Ms. Plewitt helped me develop some hypotheses about when or if I stutter when responding to the teacher's questions.

1. If I spend too much time thinking about stuttering and worrying about it before I responded, then I was more likely to stutter.

2. If I focus on my answer, sharing my ideas, and what I want to say, then I was less likely to stutter.

3. If I didn't take any think time to ease into my speech, then I was more likely to stutter.

4. If I hold my breath before I speak, I will stutter. My words might not come out at all! The pushing and pulling exertion of opposing forces between my vocal cords, lungs, and diaphragm aren't the best feeling!

That worked! I was getting used to the rhythm of easing into a bunch of correct answers!

My Math class didn't consist of me being rushed to apply a formula to solve a difficult problem. We took a second to work on calculating how frequently I was stuttering, and I noticed I was stuttering less often. It was like stopping along the way to track my progress for all the hard work we were doing! It was a nice addition to my day!

My Social Studies class was all about taking control over future events, Ms. Plewitt reminded me to make my old, negative feelings about my stutter ancient history. I was stepping into a brighter and more adventurous future.

In P.E., Coach Smith showed Ms. Plewitt and me how to be still and focus on our rhythm – our breathing. We also found the bendy bones, joints, and muscles in our body, including the lungs. We learned that we have to breath to a steady rhythm to speak to a steady rhythm, and it's okay to start over or breathe a little longer before you speak.

Mrs. Bee's music class was the best. She taught me how to use one of the strongest instruments in the human body: the diaphragm. She also taught me how to speak powerful enough for the world to listen while I'm breathing from my diaphragm and use a continuous rhythm that keeps flowing. She gave me a list of rules to follow:

"1. Bee kind to yourself

2. Bee kind to others

3. Bee patient when speaking and listening

4. Bee confident

5. Bee honest

6. Bee strong

7. Bee different

8. Bee fair

9. Bee vibrant and colorful – no monotones-laugh, sing, gargle, blow raspberries, yell, whisper, go high, go low, don't be scared to go toe-to-toe

10. BeeLieve"

She taught Ms. Plewitt and me the way to warm up our voices and capture the attention of any listener. That was BeeYoutiful!

The occupational therapist, Mrs. Schivers, came to our homeroom classes and led a presentation about zoning in. At first, I thought she was going to talk about seeing things, but she said that if we pay close enough attention to our bodies, we can see the rhythm under which they are operating. Ms. Plewitt and I learned which signals to look for when I feel nervous, scared, uptight, or calm before I spoke. I learned to listen to the signals and respond to them by doing things to relax like counting, breathing like I'm cooling off a cup of hot chocolate, moving around or stretching to loosen my muscles, or simply lying down. We learned that relaxation begins with the mind. We role played different stressful situations. The key was learning to exhale just as slow as we inhaled. Mrs. Shivers handed us a personal Zoning In color-coded measurer with the Chinese Proverb, "*Tension is who you think you should be. Relaxation is who you are*" printed on it. I felt so relaxed with her.

My favorite "genius" experience was with Mrs. Genius in Art class. Ms. Plewitt and I learned to paint the rhythmic sounds of the ocean, wave after wave. Mrs. Genius turned on the radio and instructed the class to close their eyes and listen to the sound of waves crashing, splashing, coming to shore, and receding back into the ocean for more. She then instructed us to visualize what it looked like, then make the waves our very own. She told us to open our eyes and paint that picture. She gave us a handout of vocabulary words related to oceans and told us we could even include a poem because Plutarch once said:

"Painting is silent poetry, and poetry is painting that speaks." -Plutarch

I grabbed every color of water-colored paint that I could find in the room. I painted to the rhythm of the hues that spoke to me and added the following poem:

HueMan
By Abigail Brewer

The invisible wind whispers in the air
Crystal clear salt dampens the atmosphere
White cotton candy coated clouds create dimension
Into the transparent never-ending sky blue
Peace, Tranquility
That's your Hue
I remember you
Fading into the distant deep dark cerulean
Visible silver majestic mists floating above
Boats sailing out in your open
Love
That's your Hue
I remember you

Building up to the blueish green mix of what lies beneath
The sway of your deep roots peeking through the surface
Reminding us of paradise
And who created all of this
Nice
That's your Hue
I remember you
Marine creatures living in your Pacific
Enjoying your endless and ominous boundaries
Swallowing your colorful food
Life
That's your Hue
I remember you
Crawling, rolling, and rippling
Shimmering white pinkish tinged bubble bath foamy residue
Continuously
I hear you coming
I feel the swell between your crests
Every nine to twelve seconds I can rest
Time
That's your Hue
I remember you
The anticipation of your loud crash
Splash
Blending with the sands crystalized recede
Waiting for the next one thereafter

Laughter

That's your Hue

I remember you

Golden suntanned unstable legs and feet

Standing at the shore

Rainbow painted toes running towards you

Waiting for more

California Beaches

Mom, Isabelle, Natalia

That's your Hue

Man, I remember you

CHAPTER 41

#PRACTICE MAKES...

"Hey team," I sighed.

Ms. Scott made us stay after school and practice in the auditorium to get a feel for what the real show would be like. The stage was old and carpeted with wool that looked like charcoal. The dull silver risers were surely on their last legs. I turned around and glanced at the heavy red curtains that reeked of musty mildew. The huge spread of seats that faced me when I turned back around were dingy, dirty, and almost ripped as much as the holes in my skinny jeans. The venue looked and smelled like failure to me.

"What's up Abigail. You good?" asked TJ.

His stone-washed, ripped-up denim jacket with different merch patches looked so cool. I couldn't help but to pay attention to the maroon hoodie and ash-colored skinny jeans he paired with it. He knew how to dress so well.

"Nah. Not for real." I responded.

"What's goin' on?" he continued.

"I just don't think I can do this. I stutter so much when I practice reading our poem with you all in class."

"Maybe it's because you are just reading it. I mean, do you even understand how on point the poem is? We all keep tellin' you that it's like you took the words right out of our mouths and even better, it sounds straight from the heart. That's hard to do! I'm gonna do you like Ms. Plewitt always does me and shoot it to you straight. You got this! Do like I do when I'm writing rhymes for my raps or freestylin'. Close your eyes and let the lyrics feel you. Let them feel your feelings. Get lost in them."

I wouldn't have thought TJ would have all the right things to say to me. I knew he was going to make it one day! I felt it.

"B-b-but we don't have a-any music to play while I'm reciting the poem."

"Aye yo, didn't you tell me Mr. Bee told you to ask him for anything you needed?"

Zack, Imani, and Lauryn walked up and joined us.

"What do we need from Mr. Bee?" they asked.

"A-apparently a lot. But I-I guess it's worth a shot," I said as I thought about my last personal encounter with Mr. Bee in the sixth grade. It was traumatizing. He hosted the school Spelling Bee then and mispronounced the word he told me, and I lost! Apparently, Mr. Bee was the only person who left out the 'a' in "voyage'" three times in a row and in a sentence! It turned out "voyge" isn't a word. Were the judges not listening? That still makes me mad! I hoped he didn't confuse what I need with other words.

We chatted about what we needed and practiced acting it out on stage. If we could get the props and extra stuff for our performance, it might be one of the best performances at Robinhood, if I could find my rhythm.

CHAPTER 42

#ROLL WITH IT

U p until this day, Granny never let me hang out with my friends unless she and Papa or Mama were around to chaperone. She was starting to let down her guards because I was getting older. I thought I would feel more excited to go to the Coach Lite roller-skating rink with my focus group from Ms. Scott's class. With my heart in my stomach and jittery hands, I fumbled through the colossal laundry basket of clothes Mama told me to fold a few days ago. I didn't have time for that; everything was wrinkled and worn. I couldn't go out like that. Tossing everything on the floor, I sat there and imagined a closet full of newly designed clothes. This was precisely why I wanted to be a fashion designer. No one made the colorful, cute, casual, and comfortable, sporty clothes I wanted to wear. If I had some hue of rose pink, ripped-up jogger jeans with a rose gold elastic waist and trim, a matching hoodie, and an army green jacket to pair with them, I'd be in there!

I opened Natalia's closet. She's at violin practice, so she'd never notice if anything was missing. Mama always took her shopping for new clothes because she seemed to be growing out of everything by the day, and not by height! I won't even get into the growth spurt I had this summer. Mama didn't believe me when I told her my shorts looked like something a video girl would wear, and I was flooding in all my jeans. I had to keep wearing them and embarrassing Granny at church for her to finally take me shopping. She must've figured that because Isabelle wasn't having the same clothing problems, neither was I. It's nice to be the tallest of all of the girls in the house; however, I couldn't share pants and shoes with anyone anymore.

Looking around in the closet, I believed she had some clothes lying around that she couldn't fit anymore. For the first time, I thought, I instantly became jealous of my own sister's wardrobe. Tag after tag, the smell of fresh new garments spoke to me. I felt like Mama was holding out on Isabelle and me. I snatched the army fatigue jacket off its hanger, paired it with my maroon graphic tee that read 'Blessed' and black high-waisted ripped skinny jeans. It would've been dope if I had the custom-made high-top Converse shoes that Papa ordered for me. The army camouflage, maroon heel stripe, and the word Jesus stitched into it would've set my outfit off. Every Christmas he usually let me design a pair, and he orders them for me as a gift. It's his way of allowing me to put my creative design skills to work and test them in the world. This time, he let me design a pair early because he said he wanted to get me a little something to help me through my upcoming performance. My black and rose gold, metal-studded, high-top Converse would have to do for today; however, only Jesus was going to get me through this day because He knew I couldn't roller skate to save my life!

Before I knew it, Lauryn's mom was outside the door honking her horn. Granny and Papa went out to her car and asked her a lot of questions. That was typical of them. I should've known it was too good to be true to get picked up in one clean sweep. Latching the link to my rose gold cross bracelet that matched my earrings, I saw Lauryn and Imani get out the car. Granny clearly admired their outfits because they spun around for her, which was embarrassing. Lauryn's smile told me she loved the attention. They did look cute.

"Hey, Abigail! Cute jacket! I love your jewelry," commented Imani.

"Nice kicks! Where did you find studded Converse?" asked Lauryn.

"My Grandpa found them at the outlet store over the summer. He knows I have a fetish for such shoes," I replied.

"How sweet," Imani's mom interjected as she looked at us in the rearview mirror while driving.

Soon enough, we were pulling up to the skating rink and squeezing our double-socked feet into brown, raggedy rental skates. TJ and Zach were gliding around the rink to the latest pop songs like professionals. I knew they were going to laugh at me scoot and drag myself around the walls, trying my best not to fall. I had a flashback of when I first learned to ride my bike. My mom's friend guided me for a while and let me go free on the sidewalk as soon as I found my balance. The problem was he never showed me how to break and I almost rode smack dab in the middle of traffic on a busy cross street. Thank goodness he was a fast runner and caught me seconds before what would probably would've been known as my short-lived life. Granny and Mama freaked out and barely let me ride alone again. They made me ride super slow from then on. It took Papa to remind Granny that "I'm covered" when I'm out there. I hope I'm covered on this rink today!

"Come on, Abigail. Loosen up! Skating is like hula hooping. You have to find a constant and continuous free-flowing movement in your hips to guide you and roll with it. Your legs shouldn't look like Pinocchio's before he turned into a real boy," Imani said as she looked at me and burst out laughing.

"I-I know. I-I-I'm trying," I said as I tried to take two steps forward. I felt like a robot lifting heavy metal skates while trying to maneuver across the carpet. The more I lifted my feet, the more gravity pulled them back to the floor, which caused me to lose my balance. Eventually, I fell on my butt; I hoped nobody noticed.

Lauryn helped me up, held my hand, and guided me on to the slick, round skate area. We went around twice before she unexpectedly let go of me and left me in the middle of the arena. The neon graffiti on the walls were beginning to spin. Suddenly, I felt sweaty. This was all bad! I couldn't believe she did this to me. TJ and Zach were quickly approaching me. Their light denim jeans and teeth were glowing under the black fluorescent lights. I hoped and prayed they wouldn't ask me to skate with them.

"Come on Abigail. Let's get our roll on," said TJ as he reached for my hand.

The moment of truth arrived. I thought I was going to pass out. Why did TJ ask me to go out there and make a fool of myself in front of him? An instant vision of Granny strolling in here and asking TJ who he thought he was skating with me came to mind.

"Um...I don't know," I politely replied.

Two seconds later, Zach pulled me out into the fast-moving crowd of the fearless skaters next to him and TJ. I leaned backward and forward as I tried to stay on my feet that were stuck in a 10 and 2 position while holding on to a good-sized chunk of his sweatshirt. I'm sure it looked more like he was dragging me across the floor on wheels. TJ was beside us laughing at me the entire time.

"Relax. You got this! Listen to the beat of the song," said TJ

He continued with a serious look on his face as he switched positions and skated backward to face me, "Let your arms and legs catch the rhythm. Let the wheels roll you. When you feel them slowing down or stopping, gently push off one foot at a time to get your momentum back. Then glide through it again. The trick is to start off easy. If you aren't used to it and try to rush, you will always mess up. I had to learn it the hard way. See this scar on my chin?"

A nickel-sized scar from a gash was on his chin.

"O-ouch! That must have hurt," I said.

"Look at you. You aren't even holding on to Zach anymore. See, you were thinking about it too much! Skating is just like free-style rapping, too. Just like I said about writing rhymes. Once I catch a nice beat and start to feel the rhythm, my rhymes flow. I start to think about a story I've been waiting tell or feelings I want to get out. Sometimes, I have to pause to take a breath. At other times, I have to stop to think about more lyrics. That's like taking your time to get the hang of skating until you feel ready to just go, and it's okay. The best flows come when I give myself time to think about them. I remind myself I'm free to take my time, so I don't rush, get all panicked, and mess up. I pick back up from the hook until another bar to my story comes to mind. Then I flow again and again."

TJ was making perfect sense. I was lost in everything he said, and I started to relate it to stuttering at that moment, somehow. I completely forgot I was skating for a minute. I thought when I slowly ease into speaking through relaxed breathing, my speech comes out so much smoother. It's like when I prepare to relax and give myself permission to speak at a slower rate, I don't worry about crashing and falling as much. If I hit a bump and stutter, I can get back up and easily speak again, and it's okay. I felt like TJ understood me! I thought he just taught me how to skate, too. I started grinning from ear to ear as I began to coast to the rhythm of the songs.

I spoke too soon. I wasn't expecting to fall on my butt for a second time. This time I took Zach, TJ, and two small children down with me. We sat and laughed for a second before we helped each other to our feet and gradually eased back into skating. For the first time, I felt like people weren't worried if I fell. No one was looking for me to fall. Falling is a part of the process of learning. It has to be the same with stuttering. Were people worried if I stuttered? They weren't looking for me to stutter. Did people want to talk to me, get to know me, see me get up after I fall, and keep going? It would've been so weird if I stopped talking in the middle of a stutter. I never psyched myself out about learning how to skate. I went out there, fell, and got up again. Failing never came to my mind. I didn't stop trying, so, I must look at standing in front of the school to recite my poem in the same way. Stuttering didn't mean I would automatically fail. Me not getting up to do it is failing.

I was glad we took Ms. Scott's advice about spending time together as a group outside of class to become comfortable working together. I was able to slightly understand another one of Papa's favorite sayings, "The best moments in falling are getting to experience the joy of rising." I can roll with this!

CHAPTER 43

#ASK AND YOU SHALL RECEIVE

The madness Mr. Bee warned us about was coming to fruition. Robinhood felt like a rat race. Teachers, students, volunteers, community donation drop-offs, and phone calls were more frequent in the front office. Most of the daily traffic consisted of my focus group and me. Every other day, we plead with Mr. Bee for more things. It's to the point where his secretary told us to just go back to his office because she's so tired of us bugging him with unrelenting, annoying buzzes. Mr. Bee must have been tired of us, too, because he told us to go ahead and write down what we needed and he would get it. I made sure that I didn't misspell anything on the list, too. I would've hated to be the cause of him failing to deliver us the goods because of him mispronouncing a word like he did at the spelling bee. Things were starting to look promising.

Students who participated in after-school practices flooded the evening activity buses, and the rides home became a never-ending journey of their own. This must be what show business is like.

Every evening, I finished dinner and practiced reciting my poem repeatedly. I also noticed that I was beginning to stutter repeatedly, and I didn't understand why.

I usually didn't stutter when I was by myself. I stuttered looking at myself in the mirror, in the shower, in the closet, in the backyard, in the laundry room, and even in Papa's den."

I considered giving up. I wasn't going to be inducted in the stuttering hall of fame at the show.

Tears burst from my eyes. "Lord, help me," I cried out. "You promised to be my strength. You promised to be my rock. You promised to save me from this Goliath. You promised to guide me with your light and show me the way. Send me the tools I need. Surround me with an army to help me rise up."

I threw myself on my bed and wept.

CHAPTER 44

INTERCESSION: DIAMONDS

"Abigail. Sweetie. Why are you crying? What did Isabelle do? Do I need to go snatch somebody up by the collar? What happened?" asked Papa as he ran in my room.

"I don't know," I replied while sniffing my nose. "I just can't seem to stop stuttering when I read the poem I-I have t-t-to read in-in-in front of the school."

"Baby girl. Sit up. Sit up right now. Wipe your face. Straighten up, and I want you to look at me and really listen," Papa said as he pointed his index finger at me and sternly looked at me. Nothing about this felt warm and comforting.

He continued, "Remember the diamond I gave you?"

I looked at it, "Yes Sir."

"It's sparkling now right?"

"Y-yes ssss-sir."

"How much is it sparkling?" he asked.

I interrupted, "Papa you don't get it. I-It bothers me how hard I have to work to talk! You all think I'm ssss-supposed to j-just "love my st-stutter" – like the speck in my diamond. The difference is e-e-even with a speck – a diamond doesn't have to work to sparkle! I have to work so hard to do all of these fancy things to t-try not to stutter…while I talk! And unlike diamonds, nothing about stuttering is beautiful to me!"

"Abigail, Abigail, Abigail. I know you didn't ask to be born with a stutter, but you must realize that zillions of people in this world are like diamonds. If you think about all of the diamonds that are born – it is destiny for all of them to look, feel, and be a little different than others. There are no two diamonds that are exactly alike, and even if they have the same clarity, they will never look the same to the eye. Nor will they feel the same to the person they belong to. That's what gives them their brilliant and beautiful significance to stand out from all of the others."

He continued, "Diamonds are multifaceted! They have so many glorious sides to them. Each side, every angle, and every cut is a small, intricate, and very important detail that makes up a bigger story. Without all of those facets, a diamond wouldn't be able to shine the way it does when light hits it. Simply put the fewer cuts, sides, and angles – the fewer opportunities it has to reflect light. And the less it sparkles! Abigail, you are multifaceted! You are made up of an infinite amount of God's truths, abilities, skills, talents, blessings, triumphs, victories, healings, and more. I know this because God is multifaceted, and He created you in His own image. And like diamonds, we all can reflect His magnificent light in a multitude of ways if we choose to! So, when you go out there on that stage, I want you to remember the biggest light that shines through you! Don't you let anything dark drive out your light like that barefaced lie the enemy is trying to tell you – that you can't do this. You can do all things through Christ! You can do this! You were running so well, so you know those thoughts are not from anyone on your side."

Papa was on to something and started to sound like my Youth Pastor as he went on, "You write so well. Your poems are so beautiful – well at least the ones you let me take a peek at. I am willing to put money on it that your voice is one of the greatest things about you, and somebody is after it because that's where the Most High has planted something amazing in you. Here me out. Your voice is so much more than stuttering. It's more than the audible sound that travels through your larynx. It's the resonance of your heart waiting to resonate its contents with humanity. Just think about all of the students and families who are going to feel so brave after your performance. If you don't understand what I am saying, let me break it down to you."

Grandpa knew I was lost at larynx. He spoke from his background in the Anatomy and Physiology classes he taught in the high school's P.E. and Health classes.

"The sound that is in your heart means a heck of a lot more than the sound of your voice itself. Your real voice is what you say, not the pitch, volume, or how fast or slow you speak. Your voice is one of the things that defines you! Now, look at me. You know the Lord will never leave you and He will never fail you. Your Granny and I don't constantly preach this to all of you girls because Pastor Daily does so. We've lived it and like your Granny always says, 'You're covered!' So, you get on that stage in your new custom-made Jesus Chucks that came today and let Him show the whole school those facets He created in you! He not only knows exactly what it's like to be in your shoes; He is in your shoes right with you."

CHAPTER 45

#DRESS REHEARSAL

"**G**ood morning Dragons! Today's announcements are going to be short, but sweet with no scent of defeat."

I always wondered from where did Mr. Bee get all of his one-liners?

"The show is only 5 days away, and I am sorry to announce that we have to change the location. After last night's severe thunderstorm, part of the roof collapsed in the auditorium. But never fear, the Queen Bee is here. Mrs. Bee worked her magic and dropped some honey in the ears of the local church that many of you attend and they generously agreed to let us use their space. Dress rehearsals will take place every day immediately after school until the big day. Ms. Jenkins has arranged for all of the buses to carry all of our equipment and students to the church after school. We will be coming up with a special fundraiser to raise money for an offering to give the church for being so kind. If any of you have any ideas, please do not hesitate to buzzzz me in my office! Make it a great day, Dragons!"

"I can't believe it's almost here!" said Ms. Plewitt.

"I know," I responded.

"You're ready. You're more than ready. I'm noticing that you're finding your rhythm and smoothing your words more, too. I just want you to know that I learned so much from you through all of this. I feel like I busted out of my shell this year. Your creativity is contagious, Abigail."

"Thanks, Ms. Plewitt!"

She rose to walk me to my first class.

"What is going on?" Ms. Plewitt's ears followed all of the chaos in the hallway outside of her classroom. I was right behind her. "Why is there so much whispering and stuff going on?" she asked me.

Zack and TJ were whispering to the music, drama, and computer teachers. Lauryn and Taylor were whispering to Ms. Jenkins, and Imani was whispering something about the church to Mrs. Bee. No one turned around to whisper anything to me! Were they talking about me?

I didn't have time to be worried about anything else, so I let it go. I had a bigger show to entertain.

CHAPTER 46

#ADVENTURE

It was nearly impossible to push through the busy backstage crew. I needed to get to the dressing room to meet my focus group. I glanced at the order of performances on the rustic orange program, which made my hands tremble. "There are only two performances before we're on," I said under my breath. I noticed that we were after the surprise performance entitled 'N's Vin.' I didn't have a clue who that was, but Mrs. Bee was known to get some pretty good acts to fill that surprise spot every year.

"You made it!" yelled Imani. My team threw their arms around me and handed me a folded army green t-shirt to wear.

"Just put it on over your shirt. That's what we're about to do," said Lauryn.

"Who paid for these?" I asked.

219

"Ms. Jenkins had them made for the whole school and audience members to purchase for the fundraiser."

"Ahem. Tell her!" said Imani as she looked at Lauryn.

"Wait 'til she gets it on!" commanded Lauryn.

Lauryn was smiling like she'd won the lottery, and I didn't know what was going on. I managed to slip on the shirt without messing up my perfect slicked-up edges to the ballerina bun on my head. Mama used a lot of pomade and glitter hairspray to get it to hold so I didn't have too much to worry about. I didn't even get lip gloss on the shirt.

"Ahhhh! Oh my gosh!" I screamed. "Whose idea was this? I'm so excited!" The shirt read '#Adventure' in white letters and army camouflage. "It totally matches my shoes!" I knew it was nobody but Jesus! It wasn't going to be a good day, I thought. It's going to be a God day, so I was ready!

"It was my idea to get everybody involved. Ms. Jenkins already sold out of them, but she made sure she set us five shirts aside," said Lauryn.

"I told you we got you," said TJ.

"Where is Zack?" I asked.

"He got his shirt and went to go meet the audiovisual programmer for the church. He's been meeting with him all week to get the visuals we talked about to work. He told us to tell you to watch the television prompter that will be eye level with you when you go center stage."

220

"Sure thing. As long as it's like the one we used during the run, through."

"He said it's even better," said Imani.

"Everything is going to be alright," said both Ms. Plewitt and Ms. Scott as they walked up behind me.

Taylor ran up to me from out of nowhere and reminded me of some quotes from the sci-fi book we read together. "Remember, the past can't travel with you to the future. The real treasure is in the minutes thereafter." She then hugged me and said, "Adventure is only minutes away!"

"And next up, we have a very special performance from one of our former students. Ladies and gentlemen, remain seated and remember to please silence all of your devices. This is a piece from N's vin you won't want to miss," announced Mrs. Bee.

I peeked out from backstage behind the huge, dark, and heavy velvet curtains. The stage was pitch black. All I heard was the gentle and slow touch of a bow meeting the strings of a violin. A small spotlight zoomed in on only the violin. I saw specks of resin dust in the air. The song being played was familiar but slower. I quickly picked up that it was my favorite gospel song *Break Every Chain*. It sounded better than when the choir performed it at church using the violin. The acoustics bounced off the silence in the room, which caused me to close my eyes and relax in knowing that God was with me through the performance whether I stuttered or not. The spotlight suddenly widened as the song progressed.

"It's Natalia! I'm so excited. This is too exciting! That's why she was practicing this song. God, you are sending the army. Right here, right now. I'm about to rise up!" I said to myself.

The crowd gave her a well-deserved standing ovation!

"And now we have a special grand finale for you. Instead of calling this part of the show *The End*, we decided it's the beginning of something that was discovered among the entire teacher and student body during the past eight weeks of school. We found trials, we found risks, and disaster. We found discouragement, we found creativity, we found laughter, we found unity, we found fear, and we found courage. But mostly, we found Adventure! Without further ado, please welcome to the stage – Adventure."

Blue and white floor stage strobes with sparkle lighting effects pierced through the mist of smoke at the bottom of the stage. The lights met my figure from every angle onstage. As the fog swept across the stage, the instrumental musical version of the song we selected played. TJ rippled the cymbals with his drumsticks to lead me into our poem. Imani laid in an elegant dancer's pose in an immaculate, hand- woven African wrap over her t-shirt. On stage, Lauryn sat on a stool with paint, a paintbrush, a blank canvas, and a fearless smile. I looked at the audience, at Zack in the audiovisual booth, then at Isabelle, who held up our two matching Barbie dolls to cheer me on. From what I could see, most of the audience was wearing one of the green #Adventure shirts. That included all the staff, students, and guests. I had no doubt in my mind that this was the army. I giggled a bit, closed my eyes, inhaled, exhaled, and let out a sound I'd never heard before.

The sound initiated a pulsating, reactive, audio spectrum of visual sound effects every time I spoke. I looked at the teleprompter and heart-shaped ruby red colored diamonds illuminated the screen while it displayed my words, creating a rhythm I could see, feel, follow, and speak. It was like I felt the Lord's breath in my lungs.

TJ beat the drums to the riptides of the poetry my heart sung.

Imani twirled, swirled, and grabbed hold to the story the poem told.

Lauryn brushed colors on the canvas that emulated trust.

This time, I told my entire truth through each verse and stanza. The words were theirs. The words were mine. The words were everyone's idea of me letting my light shine.

"Listen
To the picture that's being painted to my right
Look
Beyond her stars and stripes
Feel
The pain behind her brother's fight
Taste
The tears that give her water color

And that the Lord sent love to cover

Allowing her to wear His smiles

Listen

To the beat of the drum on my left

Its thunder can be heard for miles

Watch

The cymbals follow the snare

And the snare flow to his freestyles

Let it touch your heart

Because this is this the beginning of this young man's bright start

To the future God promised him

Peace, college, music, rap, words, and poetry filled with hope

Nothing to do with evil, danger, or dope

Now look a little closer to the girl next to me

Listen

To what you see

Close your eyes and feel her earth rattling stomp's vibration

Waking up this nation

Her voice is strong and beautiful

But today her arms, torso, hips, and feet

Are telling her story

of a mighty defeat

Of God's glory

Can't you see

Now look down in front of me

Listen to the effects his brilliant mind created

See the projection of his marvel

His gifts of intelligence multifaceted

The flash of his lights

Paving his way to a successful unexpected path

Now you do the math

Now look at me

What do you see

The shell that's coated in God's armor

What do you hear

No, that's not the sound of fear

What do you feel

I feel His presence near

No, that's not the body of fear

You see fear is chained to the ground

Today I came prepared

To take him down

With one weapon, one shot, and one sound

So if fear is my Goliath

Then I am David

And stuttering is the one stone that made him slain

Ending what I used to call my greatest pain

Made of broken words that are now spoken

And to many now a token

Thanks to the army that rose up around me

To set free the words bound up inside me

Wait a minute

What's that sound I hear
What's that glorious presence near
Praise God Almighty
The light called Adventure is finally here!"

Everyone in the pew stood and hugged one another, praised Jesus, whistled at us, and jumped for joy.

Pastor Daily ran on the stage and gave me the biggest high-five, grabbed a mic and belted out, "To God be the glory!"

The cheerleaders held up posters that spelled out 'Adventure'.

Mrs. Bee announced that Jilly's Cupcake Bar had generously donated hundreds of miniature cupcakes with heart-shaped diamond decorations and sparkly sprinkles on top for everyone to enjoy after the show.

Team IL Beatz gathered at the front of the stage and bowed.

That's how an amazing army and me found adventure in this thing called stuttering.

♥Abigail Brewer

#EPILOGUE

"Abigail. Come look at this!" shouted Natalia. "Look, look," she gave me her cell phone and showed me all the hits the performance received. Someone recorded and posted it on social media. The count was over 1,000 hits within 20 minutes after the show.

"P-people are posting #Adventure!" I said.

"Scroll down further!" exclaimed Natalia. I beheld a list of hashtags from those who were inspired by our performance.

#Adventure

#Stuttering is my also my Adventure

#Adventure rocks!

#Stutter with Adventure

#Stuttering was my Adventure

#Me-too

#Praise Adventure!

#You have friends who stutter!

#What an adventurous foundation-from The Stuttering Foundation

#I'd love to meet adventure! Come to Camp!

"Abigail, there are thousands of tags! One of them is even a link for other kids to go on and talk about their own adventures with stuttering!" said Natalia

"You're insta-famous!" said Isabelle!

"No. I-I think I know who answered my prayers about getting the world to see that stuttering is just a normal adventure for some of us!"

"Thank you, Jesus! Amen," I whispered to myself.

"Oh! Speaking of prayers being answered, I got approved for a home loan last week. I think I found the perfect home about thirty minutes west of Granny and Papa," Mama interjected.

"So, we're moving? When do we get to see the house?" asked Isabelle.

"Wait. I-I'm not the best with directions but wouldn't that mean we'd be o-outside of the school zone and have to go to a whole new school?" I asked.

"Possibly. Hopefully we can hold off until next semester," said Mom.

#I don't know what to say about this!

#I was just getting used to the taste of this season's honey!

#HELP

#OMG

#!%$*&@!!!

Made in the USA
Lexington, KY
09 November 2019

56767608R00133